SPECIAL MESSAGE TO READERS

THE ULVERSCROFT FOUNDATION
(registered UK charity number 264873)

was established in 1972 to provide funds for research, diagnosis and treatment of eye diseases. Examples of major projects funded by the Ulverscroft Foundation are:-

- The Children's Eye Unit at Moorfields Eye Hospital, London
- The Ulverscroft Children's Eye Unit at Great Ormond Street Hospital for Sick Children
- Funding research into eye diseases and treatment at the Department of Ophthalmology, University of Leicester
- The Ulverscroft Vision Research Group, Institute of Child Health
- Twin operating theatres at the Western Ophthalmic Hospital, London
- The Chair of Ophthalmology at the Royal Australian College of Ophthalmologists

You can help further the work of the Foundation by making a donation or leaving a legacy. Every contribution is gratefully received. If you would like to help support the Foundation or require further information, please contact:

THE ULVERSCROFT FOUNDATION
The Green, Bradgate Road, Anstey
Leicester LE7 7FU, England
Tel: (0116) 236 4325

website: www.foundation.ulverscroft.com

THE SECRET FRIEND

Sophia has a secret friend, James Dalesman, her soul mate. In their youth, the two pledged that no one would ever come between them. Ten years later, Sophia is an heiress to a wealthy estate and must provide a respectable heir to carry on the family's wealth; while no matter what James has done, his position has never been equal to hers. Can Sophia's father, society's rules, or even a war tear the couple apart, or is it their destiny to be together despite the obstacles in their way?

VALERIE HOLMES

THE SECRET FRIEND

Complete and Unabridged

LINFORD
Leicester

First published in Great Britain in 2019

First Linford Edition
published 2019

*A catalogue record for this book is available
from the British Library.*

ISBN 978–1–4448–4097–1

Published by
F. A. Thorpe (Publishing)
Anstey, Leicestershire

Set by Words & Graphics Ltd.
Anstey, Leicestershire
Printed and bound in Great Britain by
T. J. International Ltd., Padstow, Cornwall

This book is printed on acid-free paper

Prologue

Winter, 1796

Shadows surrounded Sophia as she ran
down the murky passage, cutting between
the kitchens and the laundry. This should
have been a foreign world to her were it
not for her secret friend. It was a place
where her mother forbade her to go
— ever. But tonight it was as far away as
she could get from the screams — her
mother's anguished cries, the heart-stopping,
blood-chilling sounds that ripped into
Sophia's soul. She had tried to run into
the bedchamber, tried to break through
the male barrier of her father and the
doctor, his doctor, but she was not allowed
to. Brent, her father's man, had been called,
and she had been physically restrained,
prevented from being at her mother's
side. Sophia hated him, hated men, hated
them all for their highhandedness and

cruelty. Could they not see her desperation and hear her mother's need for her?

Her father's orders were echoing in her head. 'Seize her and lock her in her bedchamber.' Then his eyes, glaring, angry, focused on her. 'Be quiet, child! Show some dignity!' He pointed an accusing finger. His words were as damning to her ears as her mother's cries. 'Let me know when it is all over,' he ordered Brent.

Whatever 'it' was, Sophia did not want to know as 'it' made her mother cry out. The doctor re-entered the room. Sophia looked imploringly at her father, yet he merely shook his head despairingly, obviously disappointed with her behaviour as usual.

Sir Kenneth Baxter-Lodge showed little emotion as he declared, 'I shall wait in my study.' He waved his man and her away as he passed by them and made his way down the stairs to his own personal sanctum, where he could at least hide away from her mama's plight.

Sophia lashed out with her heel,

wriggling free from the man's chubby hands when he gasped in pain as her bone contacted his with force. Then determinedly with a final back kick to his shins, she managed to break free. Ignoring the tears falling down her cheeks, she ran straight for the servants' passage. She didn't want to be alone. She needed James.

The floor of the servants' stairs always was surprisingly cold and hard to her silk-slippered feet. This sparse stairwell and empty corridor were bereft of any furnishings. It was not like it belonged to her home, the Hall, where she had been raised in warmth and comfort. Yet these arteries were the vessels that kept it functioning, with servants seeing to their daily chores, out of sight and mind. It was her and her mother's home; her father spent most of his time in the city. This was a strange dark place, so foreign to her. Ducking behind a pile of laundry discarded within a corner of a large stone storage room, she hid.

Sophia shivered; her nightdress was no barrier to the cold emanating from the floor and walls. Two maids ran past her carrying more water and towels. She watched the steam rise from the jugs as they went by.

Sophia reached out as another maid returned and heaped soiled linen on top of the pile of laundry. Then her hand touched something wet — a blood stain. Her mother's blood. Her own ran as cold as the stone as a gasp escaped her trembling lips. Sophia could not run away anymore.

'Grab her!' a voice shouted.

Sophia shot up. She took two steps back, but stopped with a bump as she was pressed against the damp wall. Mrs Gribbins moved forward. Brent was standing with arms folded across his body, his long coat serving to emphasise his portly build. Both disguised a bulldog-like strength.

James, the stable hand, was watching from the passage, his face showing his distress or fear; there was nothing he could do to help her. She was cornered. Like a wild animal, she fought: hands, nails and feet. Before she could escape again, Mrs Gribbins threw a sheet over her and, like a swaddled babe, she was confined. Brent picked her up and swung her over his shoulder to be taken back upstairs.

Jostled along, she realised the sounds had abated. No more screams. No more tears. Nothing. Silence ensued. An eerie silence as if . . . as if . . . Sophia's body slumped, for she too had given up the fight.

1

Summer 1806

'Sophia!'

'Yes, sir?' Sophia greeted her father in the polite, detached manner she normally used since her mother had left this world for a better place.

'I need you to make arrangements for a dinner party for my dear Cynthia on the 19th. It will be held in the garden if the weather is pleasing, or if not, in the orangery. See that there is adequate provision for ten people and room for a quartet to play for an hour. I expect that it will begin at 3p.m. and carry on until dinner. Then allow for the guest rooms to be made available and for the ladies to freshen up. The party will then continue with dinner and an evening of good humour: charades, games, and music of course. I want you to sing three songs before dinner as the guests gather, something inspiring and patriotic, and then you may dine with us before retiring. The ladies will be shown to the withdrawing room, and you shall make sure that the servants clear all away and leave everything freshly laid for morning. The men will break their fast early, as a shoot has been arranged, and the ladies will arise by the time we have returned.'

He stopped to cough and take a breath before continuing. 'Arrange for a buffet lunch to be set in the oak dining room and be there as the guests depart. I want everyone to depart at least two hours before our dinner is served, which will be set for me, Cynthia, you as usual, and our guest Mr Lucas Huntley.'

He turned away from her as the instruction had been given. She was dismissed.

'Mr Lucas Huntley?' she repeated, since she had no idea who this man was. The name meant nothing to her, as his new acquaintances tended to be fleeting or transient at best; this was not unusual. Therefore, having one man join their small family for dinner was strange.

'May I ask who he is and why he is joining us, sir?' She thought momentarily of calling him 'Father', but that word represented a distant memory, like its opposite 'Mother'. They would never fade completely if she could help it. However, now he had Cynthia, who had not only money in abundance but youth and energy. Since her arrival the previous autumn, fortunes for his estate had improved; it now thrived again and was lively with dances, gatherings, hunts and assemblies. The woman, only five summers older than Sophia, whose brain was as flighty as her manner, seemed to keep 'Sir' happy and showed no malice toward Sophia, who tolerated her arrival well as it also kept her and 'Sir' apart. This change in the family's good fortune also made Sophia an heiress of some note; though at twenty-four, one who was less likely to find a suitable match in her own eyes. However, she was still very useful as a hostess, and a lure for greedy men to flirt with the notion of acquiring her dowry and ultimately that fortune, whilst marrying into an old family name.

'He is an associate of mine. You will wear something becoming. I wish you to make an effort to be pleasing.' His attention was instantly returned to the papers in front of him. He laid the letter he had been holding down on his desk and flipped the tails of his jacket before sitting down, ready to pen his reply.

'I always aim to be 'pleasing', Father.' She watched as his head slowly lifted, his worldly eyes looking straight into her own slightly challenging ones.

'I am sure you do try, but you will wear the dress that your mother has chosen — ' He shook his head. 'That is that Cynthia has chosen for you, and make sure that you have your hair made

10

up. It is not an unbecoming shade of brown — walnut, I suppose, best describes its hue. She will see that it is decorated and tinkered with to lift its weight away from your face. Your features may be strong rather than feminine, but she will try to make them as appealing as she can. Now, I have work to do, and you have your instructions.'

Sophia did not move, but stared at the top of his head. She had been dismissed, and he had returned his attention to his papers. Strange she had not realised how his hair had thinned and was turning to strands of grey amongst his own dark brown locks.

'Why is it so important that I, who am your daughter and who serves to keep house, should appear so appealing for this dinner, sir?' she persisted, and saw that a round blotch of red had appeared on his stubbled cheek as he slowly raised his face. Brent had been remiss this morning; her father's face was usually smooth. The lines that life had etched into it over the past forty or so years could not be removed, but the growth of hair could.

'Not 'Father' this time?' He sat back, his head tilted to one side. There was almost a glint of humour in his face and voice. 'It is a long time since you used that word, Sophia. Yet we are 'sir' again so swiftly.'

'You are my father,' she answered, not moving from her stance.

'I am well aware of that, girl, but sometimes I think you forget it.' He barked his words out, showing the apparent frustration he had been holding in over the years.

Sophia's resolve wavered. 'No, sir, I . . . '

'You resent being in charge of the household. Perhaps you would like me to employ a housekeeper of higher ability to organise. Someone who Cynthia can be controlled by? For you would not have the authority as lady of the Hall. She is not worldly . . . like you . . . '

'Nor am I, Father.' Sophia stared back at him.

'You would have been left to your own choices and, besides, you are far more practical than Cynthia and not so easily controlled by the will of other people. So should I let her continue to be guided by my ungrateful daughter, who has a full complement of staff to organise and keep her days busy running the Hall, whilst I see to the business of making our estate wealthy once more, as it was in the days of my father's fathers?' He sat upright. 'Or not?'

'I had not . . . ' she began, but he was in full flow and would not be interrupted.

'You had not thought of your duties in such a light? Craving perhaps to play more the part of a lady? That is why my dear Cynthia is the delightful way she is. She has not been shown a practical life. Reality has not touched her like life has etched it into your young heart. Nor had you thought about how you are lucky not to have been sent to a convent or thrown out on the streets, girl, for your damning behaviour.'

'Father, I . . . '

'Do not even dare try to placate me on this matter. It did not work then and neither will it now.' He folded his hands together, waiting for her response. 'The memory of my daughter and heiress canoodling with a hired hand will haunt me to my dying days.'

'Father, that is the past; and besides, I never . . . ' Sophie was sure he was deliberately making more of this memory to try and control her in some way — guilt was a determined weapon. Did he want to keep her there forever in his debt?

'You never realised that I place more trust in your domestic ability here than my own delightful but inadequate wife? Or that by keeping your mind and body busy, you stand less chance of getting into trouble by the hand of a hired servant?'

'James was . . . '

14

'A stable hand,' he said flatly. 'Perhaps, Sophia, you should think a little more and at a deeper and less selfish level. You have the household accounts at your fingertips. You write your notes to the suppliers and change them if they do not meet your standards. You have my ear and you have my trust to do these tasks. How many men would trust a daughter — a woman — so? What else in God's name do you want? I am glad that you have never slipped back into your earlier wanton behaviour, so let us hope that you have outgrown it and that my feelings of shame dissipate completely. So tell me, what more can I give you, girl?' He raised his hands skyward.

'Your love,' she said without hesitation or thought. His eyebrows rose and the silence lengthened between them. Sophia dare not speak a further word. She knew she had spoken out of turn. She had never challenged him before.

He shook his head. 'You are an intelligent woman; something many of my colleagues do not even believe exists. Yet you are blind. I loved your mother dearly. Yours was not the only heart to break when she died. Yet I did not act in a shameful manner and excuse it as a comfort to my grief. Instead, I wanted to secure the future of the estate. My small family's future.'

Sophia could not prevent her head from jerking back slightly; his words felt like a slap on her cheek. 'He helped to teach me how to ride, sir.' She swallowed. 'You know this, for it was with his father and him that you left me under instruction. His family are good people.'

'Every word you utter digs you in deeper. He was a servant boy you should not even have acknowledged the existence of, and yet you were wrapped in his arms.' He shook his head. 'I only employ good people on the estate. They need to be of good character. That does not mean I want them in the family!'

'I didn't make excuses. It was out of friendship, Father, and I noticed him because he saved me from a fall when I was out riding. He saved me, Father, and . . . and . . . besides, servants are people too!'

'Now you talk like a revolutionary!' He balled his fists. The mention of the revolution made him remember the Terror in France and the tales of horror he grew up with. Now with the fight ongoing with Napoleon, he was easily riled. He shook his head. 'You admit, then, you had also ridden with him. If I had not returned early, what else would you have done with him?'

'I will ignore that question, as it does not deserve an answer, Father. He was my riding instructor and I was grateful for his bravery.' She swallowed. 'I know you loved Mother . . . ' She was whispering now, trying to restore a sense of calm between them.

'You might for the first time realise it, as I can see you have never considered these points before as you were lost to your own emotions and grief. If you had, you would not say such foolish words to me.' He sighed. 'Do not even bother trying to explain or excuse yourself. I did not believe you then and will not believe you now. James Dalesman — a common stable hand — is now serving with his beloved horses in the cavalry. Be grateful to me that I bothered to get him a position in the light dragoons due to his father's long service on the estate before him. Granted, he was good with horses, and so will use his skills to help our country fight the demon Napoleon. If he survives, he had better not show his face here again. Now, you have your instructions, and my stated faith in your ability to carry them out. You have a quest, dear Sophia, to befriend Mr Lucas Huntley. Do as I have requested.'

'A quest . . . ' Sophia repeated, ignoring the comments regarding James. She had received word from a friend of his, a lieutenant, that he was alive and well and longed to return for her once the war was won. That had been last autumn, and so she waited in hope. He would come back to her a hero with rank, and then they would be together. They were merely embracing in the stables, but that was more than enough to have had her labelled and disowned if it had not been her father who had discovered them when he returned from his ride. They had been just cuddling to comfort her when she needed someone to hold her — but they were young and happy and, foolishly, she thought, in love.

'Yes, befriend him and discover what humours him, what interests him, and report what you find out in innocent conversation back to me. Let him walk with you around the orangery or in the walled garden, if the evening is pleasant. Do not go beyond our sight,' her father said, and waved a warning finger at her. It was all Sophia could do not to scream at him, *I am innocent and have been for too many years!* What good would it do, though? She had behaved shamefully and he had seen it for himself. She owed him, for he had saved her from what could have been a ruin of her own making. Her secret friend had provided much excitement and fun throughout a bleak winter and into one spring. She had been so happy. But once seen in his presence was once too many.

'Why, Father?' Sophia asked.

'Because I ask it of you, and you are my devoted daughter, are you not?' He smiled; no answer was needed. 'Now go and do as I say, and see if you can find out what makes the man's heart beat. What is it that interests him up here, and why is he bothering to visit our estate when he is supposedly on his way down to London to set up trade in the new lands? I have heard his son's engagement was called off, but I do not know why. His son is nearly thirty, never married, and owns land in the colonies and also in London. Why then has he no wife? And, if it is possible, I would consider a match depending on what we find out about him.'

'You would send me to the colonies with a strange old man?' Sophia was appalled at the suggestion.

He laughed. 'Believe me, girl, I have been tempted by the thought. No, your cousin Annabelle needs a suitable spouse, and her mother and father have asked me to help. They also want her to move away — far away — as her temper has not improved since childhood. But she is a beauty.'

Sophia was momentarily insulted by the dismissal of the idea that she should be considered. Yet any man who would take on Annabelle would need to have a hard heart and something wrong with him. Beauty she might be, but to have her as a life's companion . . . 'Why do you not ask his father when you see him?'

'Because I want to know the man's weaknesses, and I believe he will defend his son to me; but you may very well be able to ascertain something in innocent conversation with that amazing sixth sense of yours that you have developed over the years. So catch his fatherly eye. Find out if his son is worthy; his business affairs I can find out about easily, but I would understand the man better. Now go, or you will have nothing ready and Cynthia will have a fit of the nerves.'

Sophia left him, strangely excited at the prospect of meeting Mr Huntley and setting about her quest. Perhaps her father had finally forgiven her the shame of her youthful indiscretion — perhaps!

2

Sophia's arrangements worked to perfection. The first day went as she had planned, and the guests all seemed entertained and satisfied. More importantly, her father was.

'Sophia!' Cynthia almost ran along the corridor after her dinner. She was, Sophia thought, like a wood nymph slightly worse for wine perhaps. Her youthfulness still shone in her rosy cheeks and happy smile. Sophia liked her even if it did feel disloyal to her mother's memory, but this woman had brought life back to the Hall and to her father.

'Is something wrong, Cynthia?' Sophia asked, knowing if there was, she was sure that she would be able to correct it in minutes for her. Cynthia's dilemmas were rarely very challenging.

'No, all is excellent!' She kissed Sophia on the cheek. 'Thank you,' she said, and was about to run back when Sophia stopped her.

'Cynthia!' Sophia said in an inspired moment. 'Who is Mr Lucas Huntley?' she asked, and saw her smile spread to her eyes.

'Mr Huntley is an old friend of my father's. Kenneth has invited him here because he is interested in investing in a venture with sheep.'

Sophia's puzzled expression spread naturally into a smile. 'With sheep?'

'Yes; he has invested in land in the colonies, and your father has lots of good sheep. If old man Huntley is willing, your father's stock will help start a new and hardy breed out there. Only, he always plays hard to get, so your father wants you to play to his weakness . . . ' Cynthia bit her lip and raised eyebrows at Sophia.

Cynthia was not quite so blinkered in her vision, Sophia realised, as she appeared to be. 'He likes good dinners?' she asked, hoping it was not young female company that was his weakness.

'You are so innocently sweet at times, Sophia. He likes to be charmed and flattered by a pretty young woman. I am married and can only, and rightfully, tend to your father's expectations. But you may hang on his every word, laugh delicately at his every quip, and make sure that his plate and glass overflow satisfactorily. Besides, he has an eligible son!' She actually winked at Sophia.

Cynthia gave her a quick pat on her shoulder, then drifted back to her guests. Sophia sighed. She would rather organise a banquet that she did not have to attend herself than fawn over such a man as Mr Huntley Senior. What if he decided that she would make a good companion for his old age? She hoped beyond hope that he was married to a Mrs Lucas Huntley whom he adored. For one thing, her father would not approve of her marrying new money and not old; but she suspected more than this that he would not want to lose her from the

Hall. That suited her fine, because one day, on a day of her own choosing, she would leave.

★　★　★

The horse began to limp and Lucas Huntley began to curse. If it was not enough he had been sent to this godforsaken part of the country when he could have been on his way to oversee the move to the colonies, he now had to stand in for his father as if he had any interest in sheep, wool or their masters. His father had convinced him they could live like dukes in the Australias where money, like the country, was new and had more import than a man's ancestors. Now even the horse had seemingly given in. Lucas jumped down and steadied the animal. His annoyance turned to concern when he saw that there was a small cut on its fetlock that looked quite deep. He patted the animal's neck — it was hardly its fault — and decided that he would walk the last mile to town, where he would have it tended to and rent another one to ride to this Fenton Hall.

The day was pleasant enough, and as he made his way down from the moor road to the market town of Gorebeck, he stopped to admire the view. The church steeple and bridge over the river seemed to mark the central point. It was a crossroads; this town appeared to be growing, expanding along the vale. Even in his reluctant state, he had to admit that on a day as sunny as this one, it did present a unique natural beauty.

★ ★ ★

James limped as he climbed down from the coach. It was a blessing that he had made it back to Gorebeck in one piece — well, almost.

'Your bag, man,' the driver shouted down as he untied it from atop the coach. 'Ask the lad over there to give you a hand with it.' The driver dropped the leather holdall from the full height of the coach. Fortunately there was nothing wrong with James's arms, and he broke its fall before it fell to the ground. He nodded at the man and glanced at a boy leaning against the inn's wall, sucking on a clay pipe as if he was older than his young years. James wanted to tell him not to try and grow up too soon, because he would be snapped up to fight in a war on foreign soil where his chances of survival would be poor. Taking the king's shilling made young men, not more than boys, feel brave until they saw the reality of blood-spilling war — not heroic; for the likes of him could not purchase an officer's commission. James had been fortunate to have been raised up — one brave act which was in his case acknowledged — so rare; but he had been fortunate and blessed.

James wrapped his greatcoat around his uniform and picked his bag up in one hand as he manoeuvred his leg around it with the aid of a caned stick in the other. This was not how he had wanted to return to his love, at last. But at least his situation was only temporary. So he limped toward the inn. The lad jumped to his aid.

'I can do that, sir,' he said proudly.

James noticed a stranger entering the town looking much the worse for wear. 'No doubt you can, but I think that man may need your help more than I.' James pointed at the old stone bridge that crossed a river by the Norman church. A tired-looking figure was walking a limping horse over it.

'Right, sir.' The lad ran off.

James entered the inn, resting on a settle for a moment as he readjusted the strapping on his calf. How he had wanted to do that for so long on the long painful journey up from Hull. Each jolt had taken its toll.

When he approached the innkeeper, he discovered he was not alone.

'Can I help you, gents?' the man asked.

James Dalesman and Lucas Huntley

answered in unison. 'I'd like a room, please,' they both said, and then both looked at each other and nodded as they acknowledged the other's presence.

'Very good,' the innkeeper said. 'That will be a shilling and fourpence for sharing. Blankets included, food not.'

Both blurted out that they had meant to have separate rooms.

'Sorry, but rooms are all taken except for the last one overlooking the street. It's me best one, hence the cost.' The man shrugged his shoulders, glancing from one to each other as if he was wondering which or if both would take the room.

'Is there another inn?' Lucas snapped.

'Well, yes. Although I say it meself, ours is the best; but you may find more female companionship down at the Rabbit and Hare.' He sniffed in genuine disapproval.

'I'll take the room,' James said as he looked at the stranger and raised his brow.

'That will be two shillings for one, or

someone else will be able to share it with you should they need a room.'

'My horse is stabled here. I'll share one night and will be moving on in the morning,' Lucas said.

James nodded at the stranger. It was far from ideal, but hopefully he would be able to find an old friend in the morning and then he would not need to stay in town all alone. After spending years with his men in a unit, it seemed strange to be suddenly cast adrift. The thought of seeing Mrs Gribbins again made him smile, but it was the thought of seeing his Sophia again that pleased his heart greatly.

* * *

There was an awkward silence as the two men were left in the room and stared at the bed. Huntley lifted the blankets. 'Well I've stayed in worse,' he said as he dropped them back down.

James stared out of the window at the church across the road. If they could only walk down the aisle with her father's blessing, he would look after Sophia well. Realising that his roommate had made comment, he turned around and sat down on the window seat, grateful to rest his leg.

'I can say I definitely have,' he said drily, and saw the man stare at his uniform as his greatcoat fell open.

'You are recently returned?' Lucas Huntley asked James.

James nodded, wondering who the man was. 'You are — ?'

'I'm Lucas Huntley,' he said, placing his bag on the floor.

'Are you travelling through, or here for a purpose?' James asked, his curiosity aroused by the man's edginess.

'I have business nearby, once I hire a new nag, and then I will see if I can be on my way tomorrow. Are you from around here? Sorry, I didn't catch your name.'

'Lieutenant James Dalesman of the 29th — '

'A cavalry man?'

'Was.' James tapped his leg gently.

'Shot in action?'

'Broken in the fall when they took out my horse.' James shrugged. It was still a painful memory.

'You were lucky it was not you who was shot. Your father will be most relieved it was the beast that fell in action.'

'No, he won't,' James said, and watched the stranger take out a better jacket and shirt than the ones he was wearing, and flick out as many creases as he could. He glanced up at James's comment. 'He died many years ago,' he added.

'My apologies. I presumed it was he who bought your commission.'

'No one bought it for me. I earned it,' James replied, and tried to take the bitter edge out of his voice. He had been raised from the ranks after saving the supply wagon from an ambush, risking his own life to give the warning. He looked at his leg. He had had dreams of climbing much higher in the army's rankings, even if realistically he knew that prejudice against his origins would no doubt prevent that happening.

'My apologies again,' Lucas said, and smiled pleasantly. 'I have never shared a bed with a hero before.'

'I'm no hero. Right place, right time, simple as that.' He hoped beyond hope that his rank and his letter of recommendation from his colonel would be sufficient for Sophia's father to cease from shooting him on sight and at least consider him worthy of rejoining the estate — they were the only sense of family he had left; or be allowed to join the workers again in a position more befitting a man who had served than that of a mere stable hand.

'I think perhaps you are being modest. I, on the other hand, have not served. I am an only son of a self-made man who would set up a life far removed from the troubles over here. Not exactly the desires of a patriotic hero, but definitely the mind of a man who knows how to survive. However, I will not if I do not make myself presentable and ride over to Fenton Hall . . . '

'Fenton Hall?' James stood up. He looked at this man in a different light. He was a few years his senior, definitely able to pay his way, not ungainly in looks, and yet was preening to arrive at the Hall.

'You know it?' Huntley stopped flicking out his jacket and glanced at James, his attention and curiosity obviously roused.

'Yes, I am going there tomorrow as soon as I have arranged transport.' James felt odd sharing this information with the stranger, but the man immediately smiled back at him.

'Then you must arrive with me. Instead of a horse, I shall rent a gig, and you must come as my guest.' Lucas Huntley seemed much happier at the possibility.

'As your guest? Is that acceptable or

expected?' James asked. He was tempted to go along with the man's request, but was unsure if he would then make the entrance he hoped for, or if he would be shot in his good leg for his insolence at presuming he would be made welcome.

'I insist!'

'Very well.' James nodded. What had he to lose? It might well be a God-given opportunity, so why not grasp it with both hands?

Huntley swung around. 'I am invited tomorrow for dinner. You will arrive as my guest, and I will not hear another word from you on this. You have made what was to be a drag of a day into one where the evening shall have some entertainment, as you have more up-to-date news of how things fare over there than we do here.' He looked optimistically at James.

'Very well,' James said, and realised the evening Huntley envisaged could indeed be more entertaining than his new friend could ever imagine.

'Good,' Huntley slapped his back and

announced. 'I shall make enquiries and ready a gig for the morning. I will send the lad over to let them know I shall arrive with a war hero as a companion!'

'No, please, you must not. Please . . . '

'Leave everything to Lucas!' the man snapped back at him, wagging a knowing finger as he left the room. James could hear his footsteps running down the wooden stairs.

What had he done? Where would he put himself if Sophia hated him for nearly causing her ruin? Had he thought this return through at all? No! The truth was he had nowhere else to go, and he had been kept alive by the image of the young woman, his secret friend whom he adored, who had been out of his reach before he had a commission and a letter to say how grateful the regiment was for his bravery and diligence. Was it enough? Would it ever be? Then there was the Spanish gold . . . but that was a different story.

3

Sophia stared at her reflection in the looking-glass and realised that Cynthia had created an image of the daughter of a household of some wealth and note. She knew it was her reflection, but took a few moments to realise that she was actually quite pretty and not so plain. Her hair was not the fiery colour of Cynthia's with eyes that sparkled all day long with life and mischief. Sophia's were a deep blue and often reflected the depth of her thoughts. It was all she could do not to let the moisture spill into tears of joy, as for once she did not look practical and serious but feminine and fun. The immaculate curls that covered part of her forehead had been lifted above her head so that she was crowned by a cascade of dark brown ringlets. Sophia smiled, as she now naturally stood tall and proud. The golden threads that were woven through the sapphire ribbons complemented the floral embroidery on her matching silk gown. It too flowed down from the high waistline to the floor. The swoop of the low neckline above made her blush slightly, but it suited her full bosom and shapely waist. However, she would definitely have to remember to keep her back straight at all times. The pearls that rested around her neck were held by finely crafted leaves of gold and a sapphire plait of velvet.

Enough staring, she admonished herself. It was time to go and prepare to meet their guests. First she would ensure her father approved of Cynthia's choice of dress for her. He too may have quite a shock when he saw her — or she hoped that he would.

She made her way to his study. It was the place he inhabited most. Taking in one last deep breath, she held her shoulders back and tilted her chin up slightly before striding purposefully inside the very masculine room. Sophia hoped that her appearance would provide a stark and surprising contrast. He needed to realise that she was more than just his daughter who could run his home, but was a woman in her own right.

'Father,' she said lightly as she entered, closing the door behind her. She did not want Cynthia to swoop in and break this moment.

'What is it, Soph . . . ' His words stopped as he raised his head and saw her standing before him.

She slowly smiled back at him. It had worked, and he was definitely surprised. 'Do you think I am appealing enough, Father?' she asked innocently.

'You look quite stunning, my dear. In fact, for a moment I could have believed you were your mother.' He stood up. 'You would make her very proud,' he added. He moved around the desk to stand before her. His light kiss on her forehead as his hands cupped hers was the most intimate gesture she could remember ever sharing with him. 'Perhaps Cynthia may have excelled herself this time and taken my instructions a little too literally. Maybe you should . . . '

There was a knock on the door. It seemed to shake her father out of this moment of genuine affection. He stood back from her and snapped out one word: 'Yes!' His usual businesslike tone had returned, the moment of affection broken, but at least Sophia realised that for once she knew his true thoughts.

'A gig is approaching, sir,' Brent said, 'with two gentlemen upon it. Mr Huntley and his friend the war hero, his lieutenant guest, I presume, sir.' The man's face was somewhat perplexed. Sophia knew he did not like surprises such as unexpected arrivals whom his master did not even know. It was as if he guarded the Hall like a bulldog. Sophia thought it quite sweet, and wondered if her father realised how much their home meant to the man.

'Very well,' he said. Brent left them alone. Her father nodded at her. 'You are indeed appealing enough. Any more so and I fear I would have to keep you from their view. Now go to Cynthia; make sure she is prepared, and join us, as we will be shortly ready for dinner.'

'Yes, Father,' she said, and saw him smile from eyes to his lips. The affection had instantly returned.

'Good, daughter. Any man would be proud to call you such, and I certainly am. Who knows — I may set Annabelle's needs aside and consider the man for you.'

Sophia gave in to a momentary childish impulse and hugged him, hoping that he would not change his first plan — she had no wish to be matched. Before she embarrassed him further, she left him with a happy heart, believing that for once he had truly left the past behind them. She yearned to see James again when he returned from the fighting; but first she needed this time of mutual respect to share with her father before her dearest friend — her love — could re-enter their lives with even a chance of being accepted by her family.

James' resolve began to falter when the gig pulled up outside the main door of the Hall. This was not the view of it he was used to. He automatically felt as though he should take the horse and gig around to the stables, but his leg ached when he stood, so he knew it would not have been a good idea anyway. Should he have confided in his new 'friend' that he had once worked here before? He had been used to sharing a billet with his men, and so sharing a room with a respectable stranger had been no hardship. Huntley had been civil enough and did not snore, which was a small blessing, as James needed a clear head for this visit to stand a chance of passing off amicably.

Then perhaps the stranger was treating him with the respect afforded to a gentleman, and he was right to. James had become used to it from his men if not from some of his superior officers. In the army, money paid for their rank and not experience.

Mr Lucas Huntley stepped down first as a footman steadied the horse, and then James in his uniform and carrying his cane. He carefully placed his foot on the mounting step, balancing himself on the seat rail whilst quickly transferring his weight to his good leg on the ground.

'Please come this way.' The portly form of Brent the butler arrived and gestured for them to go inside. He smiled at both of them, but James had not been instantly recognised. Or could it be that he was now a few inches taller, his muscle that of a man and not a strap of a lad? The lines on his forehead were etched out due to the visions of battle, as opposed to a smooth youthful clean skin that revelled in the outdoor life and the joy of tending the animals in his care. He had intended to shave before the visit, but in the end he decided to trim it as he had become used to its feel.

Huntley gazed around him as they passed between the two Grecian-style columns that framed the doorway.

Inside, it was obvious that the ornate columns had been added onto the original facade, for the old oak that formed the great staircase ascended to a drawing room above. It looked as if at one time even a carriage could have entered the entrance hall for its passengers to alight in the shelter of the ornate home. This family must have accrued wealth from centuries ago. He looked around and wondered if it was currently receiving monies through the trade. He hoped that William Wilberforce and his followers would succeed in the abolition of the abhorrent slave trade. If so, families like this one would have to turn their business acumen to new more humane ventures.

His attention returned not to the overall wealth, but specifically to the intricate Brussels tapestries which hung on the walls of the staircases. James watched with interest as Lucas also took time to take it all in. He was used to a comfortable life, but obviously not so grand a one as this.

James had never seen this part of the building, but on occasion he had been allowed to cross the older stone hall to the second set of servants' passages, even though his place had been in the large stables at the back of this Jacobean stronghold and, if he was lucky, the kitchens. The family had done well to escape the wrath of the government, for it was well known locally that they had hidden priests and Jacobites in the place over the centuries. Yet they had survived as a family, when their causes had not.

'Ah, Lucas!' Sir Kenneth Baxter-Lodge appeared at the top of the stairs with his arms raised to greet his guests.

The man's voice nearly caused James' already unsteady steps to falter further as they were greeted. He instinctively studied the tapestry next to him, as he was slower to ascend to the drawing room's doorway than the active and fitter man.

'Thank you for inviting us, Sir Kenneth,' Huntley replied. 'My father sends his apologies that he could not arrive in person.'

'You are more than welcome. I thought for a moment that Lucas Senior had found the elixir of youth!' He laughed heartily. 'You are more than welcome. Please go inside.' He ushered Lucas through the open doorway and into the room.

James thought that it was better that the initial shock of his arrival and possible ejection from the Hall should happen here.

'Any hero of our country is forever welcome in my home, Lieutenant.' Sir Kenneth's voice seemed to bellow off the stone walls; or was it James' own conscience that amplified those words in his head? Last they met, he had been lucky to receive one strike on his back from sir's crop and not been beaten until the skin had been removed from it.

'Thank you,' James replied, still plucking up the courage to look Sir Kenneth in the eye. He wondered if his leg would be up to another knock should he find himself thrown bodily back down to the entrance hall. He really had not thought this through.

'I see you admire our family's taste in decor,' Sir Kenneth continued unabated, and walked down the few stairs to his side. Huntley had carried on into the drawing room as requested, to be greeted by Cynthia, who had arrived through the gallery entrance at the opposite end. James could hear their light chatter. So he had remarried — to a lively sort, it seemed by the tone of the laughter and good humour that was coming from inside the room.

Where was his Sophia? A thought made his blood turn cold — what if he was too late and she had been married off? It would not be unusual, and her desires would not be taken into account.

Sir Kenneth continued, 'My ancestor Lord Broderick Baxter-Lodge acquired them in France around 1640 something or other, when serving as a representative of Charles II in Versailles. We have a long and troubled history, but such is the way of stately affairs.' He shrugged as if such statements were common enough.

James looked up at Sir Kenneth, who momentarily was still staring at the tapestry. 'I should be able to bring to mind what it is about, but it has been so long since I really looked at them that I cannot remember. Strange, you pass them by daily like so many of the trinkets we posses, but I never really stop and admire any of them.' He chuckled. 'Let the women understand and fuss about such things. We have estates to run. So where do you hail from, sir?' He looked at James fleetingly, but his eyes did not linger.

'Sir . . . ' James waited until he had the man's attention. He needed to look him in the eye and judge his response.

After a moment of further reflection Sir Kenneth stared at his face, studying his eyes. 'Have we been introduced before?' he asked. 'You seem familiar to me, and yet I cannot quite place you . . . Did we meet last summer in Harrogate? The races, perhaps — are you a gambling man? No, of course not. You are newly returned, so you wouldn't have been there. Forgive me. Perhaps I know your father?'

'Indeed, we have met, and you knew my father very well. The connection is through horses, your horse . . . ' James began; but Sir Kenneth, remembering where they were, placed a hand on his shoulder and gently turned him towards the drawing room.

'My manners are at fault here; you should come and enjoy my home. Any man who has been rewarded by a commission has many a story to tell . . . and I want to hear as many as possible.'

James stood firm, careful not to teeter backward on the step when Sir Kenneth moved forward and he did not. 'Sir, it is I who owe you greatly, as does all my family, especially my poor father who passed away whilst I was serving. Graham Dalesman was a true God-fearing man who served you well with love and dedication.' James swallowed, then quickly added, 'I have a letter of recommendation from Colonel Ronald Preston, who asks that you reinstate me in a position of trust here, whilst I heal from my wound.' James swallowed again, his mouth becoming dry, and tried to balance his stance evenly. He had fought in battles and not been as fearful as he was facing this man now. He wanted Sir Kenneth's respect. To be acknowledged as a man worthy of at least sitting at his table, if not the hand of his daughter — yet. The war was far from won, and he would mend and return and climb higher up the ranks one way or another.

'Of course. But we can talk of such things later . . . ' Sir Kenneth stopped. 'What do you mean, reinstate you here? Dalesman . . . You are that lad . . . ' The tone in his voice had changed.

'It is I, sir, Lt. James Dalesman. I served in the Light Dragoons to prove myself worthy of your forgiveness, and hope that this rank and the recommendation will stand in my stead of good character. I was very young when I left here, but I am a man full grown now who has fought in battles, crossed enemy lines and saved my battalion from starvation. Will you excuse my rather clumsy reappearance, as I only met Mr Huntley in Gorebeck yesterday and he insisted that I come here with him?'

James could not read the emotion that was crossing Sir Kenneth's face. Was it shock, disbelief, or fresh cold anger? He realised that he would soon find out.

Sir Kenneth just stared at him blankly as if his appearance was incomprehensible.

'I see I have made an error of judgement. James tried to pull away from his grip that was gradually becoming firmer. 'I should have seen Mrs Gribbins first and entered at a time and place more fitting.' James looked down and began to edge his way around, ready to carefully descend the stairs. His leg hurt. The jostle of the journey of the previous day had made it ache so. He wished he could sit down in the drawing room and relax where the atmosphere seemed to be filling with geniality, but Sir Kenneth's hand gripped his shoulder.

'You have arrived here as my good friend's son's guest — a hero! Tell me, does he know of your connection to the Hall?' he asked quietly.

'No, sir; we are newly acquainted. I merely explained that I was to present myself here, as I had a letter from my colonel and he insisted we arrive together.'

'Good. Then he will not know of it, now or ever. He will remain here with you, and you will enjoy my food at my table. I take it you know how to behave in respectable company?' His eyes glared into James'.

'Yes, sir,' James answered honestly. He was not insulted, as it was a fair comment to ask a stable lad.

'Good! I will talk to you on your own once my business with Lucas is done. Do not do anything to sour it, my lad, or you will not enjoy being a hero for long!' His words were quietly spoken, but with such a sharp tone that James did not doubt that he meant every one.

'Of course, sir,' he said.

He felt the firm slap on his shoulder and realised it was harder than appropriate, but as he began to climb the last few stairs he saw a vision of perfection waiting for him at the top. Sophia appeared in the doorway of the drawing room, and James missed the top step and nearly tripped up. Sir Kenneth's grip tightened, preventing James from tumbling down into oblivion.

'Good God, man!' Sir Kenneth snapped. 'Compose yourself.'

'Yes, sir,' an embarrassed James replied, and stood proud as he admired the beauty that Sophia had become.

'Mr Huntley, I was not aware you were in the army,' Sophia said innocently.

'He is not, Sophia,' James responded, and saw the recognition on her face.

'James!' she said, her eyes as blue as the dress that flattered her colouring to perfection, along with her complexion and her figure, James thought.

'Lt. Dalesman is Mr Huntley's guest, Sophia. You will act as if he is a stranger to you and compose yourself.' Her father's warning was heeded as she nodded her assent, but James had seen his Sophia's eyes shine and her cheeks colour delicately. He knew she was still his, but hoped that her father was not aware of this, as now he himself saw Huntley in a different light — a contender or enemy.

4

Throughout dinner, it was Mr Huntley who was the quieter of the two gentlemen as the family asked questions of James. It was as if he was being cross-examined on the state of the conflicts. Sophia secretly hung on his every word, but tried not to comment or stare, as she asked Lucas questions about his preferences for the food, the state of the roads, his travels, anything to try and initiate a conversation that would engage her attention.

'Mr Huntley, I hope your father is well?' Sophia asked as she turned to him again trying to find anything out that may interest her father. It was supposed to be Mr Huntley Senior who she was to take a turn around the orangery with, not the younger, more handsome and very eligible son. But then James had returned to her

— sitting at their table — a hero! Sophia could hardly comprehend this surprising turn of events, and she was dressed to perfection to impress the wrong man. Then she remembered that it was Lucas who had an engagement that had fallen through, so there was a dark secret to reveal if she could. Yet, she ached to be alone with James to find out why he limped and how, or if, he had changed from the sweet boy she knew. Surely war embittered men. On that note she avoided eye contact with her father, who seemed to be dealing with the situation in a very calm manner.

The seating was a little awkward; Sophia was between her father and Lucas Huntley, while James sat opposite between Father and Cynthia. Cynthia had thought a round table would be more apt than that of a square or rectangular one because they were a group of five. It was unusual, yet worked well, and also meant that Huntley could also converse with Cynthia easily. Sophia was determined to keep her eyes from taking in every rugged and handsome feature of her long lost friend. How ironic that just when her father had forgiven her the transgression, James should return — it had to be the hand of fate showing them the way. Her father seemed determined to hook James' attention, and she hoped he realised that she had shown little or no interest in him, doing as he bid and being appealing to Lucas Huntley instead.

'Yes Father is well, but our new venture has tied him to London for longer than he had expected. He will of course be seeing you all before we depart. He will make it a priority, I am sure.'

Lucas sipped his wine. He looked at her and smiled, as he had frequently throughout the meal. His thigh occasionally, accidentally, touched hers. She acted as if she had been totally unaware of it, but the strange sensation that she experienced was very distracting.

'What brings you all the way up here to our humble part of Yorkshire?' she gently persisted. Sophia was aware that her father was also glancing her way, even though James was still answering his last question on the effect of the death of Prime Minister Pitt at the beginning of this year. The previous autumn's victory at Trafalgar had been saddened by the loss of Admiral Nelson. It was indeed a heavy question, but her father was watching her and Huntley and just nodding to James' optimistic, yet somewhat profound, words. It seems they were each listening to the other's conversational partner.

'Well, I had to go to Newcastle sealing up an old family business and selling off the assets, and then word spread of a beautiful lady who was the daughter of my father's good friend, and I could not keep away.' He smiled at her, while she blushed slightly and chanced a glance at James, but she noted he was not smiling at all at the comment.

Sophia was humoured at the compliment, but she was not taken in so easily by such honeyed words. She had spent too long watching the ways of social gatherings from a position that was akin to a bystander, as Cynthia adored being the centre of attention along with the wives of their guests.

'You are too kind. When do you leave for the colonies?' she asked directly.

'Ah, my dear Sophia, you are not to worry on that score, for I shall need to talk further to Lucas, so I insist that our guests stay with us a while. I will have Brent send for your things from the inn and have the gig returned. James, you will take the opportunity to rest that leg of yours, and I will have Dr Aimes sent for to make sure all is well.' Her father was not asking but telling them what he expected to happen.

'That is very generous of you, sir,' James said. He genuinely looked surprised.

'I shall read what the good colonel has to say in your letter,' he added. 'Then we shall talk again.'

Lucas sat back. 'This has been a most

remarkable meal. I would suggest that I ride the gig back to town and settle my affairs. But I would be happy to rejoin you in a couple of hours. I have a lame horse in stabling there, and if I could borrow one of yours, I would bring both back with me. Perhaps your stables would provide a better place for it to recover, whilst we continue discussing my father's proposal after a good night's rest.'

'Very well.' Sir Kenneth stood up. 'Brent, see that Lucas has everything he needs.'

'I will be back before you miss me.' Lucas stood up, excused himself to Cynthia, then turned to Sophia and smiled sweetly down at her.

He was certainly confident, she thought. Once he had left the room, Cynthia saw him out. Three people were seated at a half-empty table looking at each other with a growing silence between them.

'You must excuse me, Father, for I must . . . ' Sophia decided to break it first.

'Stay there, Sophia.' Her eyes met

James' for the first time since they had sat at the table.

'You two are nothing to each other. I will have this understood. Dalesman has earned my gratitude for the way he has bettered himself and served his country. But you are an heiress — and you, Lieutenant, are below her rank. I have made this clear now as I do not want history to repeat itself. That would result in your expulsion from your rank and yours from this home. Much as I love my daughter, I will not excuse such betrayal ever. Do not break my trust in either of you on this, or I will break you both.'

Sophia's sharp intake of breath echoed even in her own ears, for this was no idle threat; and she could tell James also understood this too by the crestfallen look in his eyes.

'You may go, Sophia,' her father declared, and sat back in his chair as she departed without further word.

'James, I want you to walk straight again, so I will pay for your leg to be given the best of attention. I owe it to my country — if not to you, then to your father. You were young and foolish once. Now you need to be realistic, mature and brave. Put all notions behind you and I shall find you a suitable bride if you so wish, in time.'

James nodded. 'It is more than I deserve. You have my undying gratitude. However, I will not burden you with finding a match for me. I will marry for love or I will not marry at all.'

'Oh, how war has failed to dampen that romantic soul. You will have to cap it, man, for I mean every word I said. Now, young man, I will have you attended properly, or Mrs Gribbins would never forgive me; and that would grieve me, for she has been here many a year.' He winked at James, whose spirits lifted at the mention of the woman who had acted as a mother to him when his own died.

James stood up, but his leg had had enough and nearly buckled under his weight.

'Good God, man! You are suffering

and still you do not say. Brent! Judd!'

A flustered footman arrived. 'Mr Brent has just left, sir,' he said.

'Yes, yes, I know that. Get a couple of men and have Lt. Dalesman carried to his room. Make haste and send for the doctor — send the carriage.' Cynthia, who returned when Sir Kenneth shouted for the servants, stood watching, most concerned while James held onto the edge of the table and he lowered himself carefully back into the chair. He had not realised until he moved that all was not well with his leg. He had become used to the constant nagging pain.

'Cynthia, when the men arrive, have him lifted in the chair carefully up the stairs to the Willow Room. Now, excuse me, as I must see Huntley before he sets off.'

'I — ' James began to protest.

'You, boy, will count your blessings and shut that mouth of yours. You may be about to be saved from a life as a cripple, but you keep your own counsel, understand me? Do not let me down, and your future will be secured.' He marched out of the room before James could respond.

'Very well,' he whispered, and tried to smile at a very attentive Cynthia.

5

Lucas Huntley left the Hall temporarily as a happy man. This was a feeling he had not experienced for nearly a year. He had now met the woman he would marry and carry off to the New World. His mind was set on it. She had beauty and intelligence — a rare commodity in any woman, but to be his partner she would need that. Her father would be pleased, for he dearly wanted to expand his income and wealth overseas; his own father would be delighted that he could finally make up for the troubles of his past engagement. He was lucky not to have been thrown into prison for breaking his vow, but what he had discovered was too much to bear. Yet to disgrace the girl in public was beneath even him, so a rake and rogue he had to be.

He smirked; it was a label that

appealed to him anyway. It made him more effective in business, as he was seen in a more formidable light — when he gave a hint of menace to one of his debtors, miraculously they now paid their dues. Who would care about a broken engagement where his destiny was headed? In the New World he would be a master of all; new money would become the established gentry — a whole fresh start.

This man James was an asset. A hero had returned with him to occupy the father at the table — a valuable distraction as he concluded his father's business. Sophia had not even given the poor chap a second glance throughout dinner. She obviously found his own wit more engaging than the bravado of a fool in uniform — cannon fodder. James would no doubt go back for more once he was well. His type needed to do the honourable thing and then revel in their suffering, retelling tales of blood and lost limbs and their victories. To what end? Napoleon would win, he had the vision to carve out an empire, just as he, Lucas Huntley, would as governor, in time, of a new and fresh land. So their family would get away from the stench of old money and begin new dynasties in a far-off land where the sun shone and bitter winters were miles and seasons away.

He breathed deeply. He had thought to pick a girl from the lower ranks, still fresh and hardy, but now he could see that would be folly. He would have one who looked strong and slightly more mature, who would cope with the change and the demands made upon her. For beautiful as Sophia was, unlike her mama, she had depth. His path was set, his mind made up. He would spend a week perhaps wooing her and toying with the father, and then ultimately relent on his wishes so long as Sophia was part of the bargain.

How sweet victory was, he thought as he collected his bag and horse, held its reins in his hand and rode in the direction of the Hall. It was more than he could have imagined when he set out to this godforsaken cold region of their damned country. But like his new friend, he would become his own hero; he would rescue Sophia and take her far away. Her life would begin again, and their offspring would be the first to inherit the Huntleys' estates. At last he would not be a disappointment to his father.

He glanced at the Norman church and chuckled. What was he thinking? Was he beginning to believe in a god, the one God, or was he just seeing opportunity and taking charge of his own destiny? He smiled and carried on. It was the latter; for what god let his minions die in such numbers on foreign soil? He kicked the horse on to make good a deal and secure his future.

★ ★ ★

James flinched in agony as he was moved up the stairs. Every jolt seemed to send a sharp pain down or up his leg.

Once in the beautifully decorated room, he was lifted onto a four-poster bed. He closed his eyes as his body finally stilled, but the pain continued. Something had definitely gone wrong with his wound. It was all he could do not to weep with the fear of losing his limb. He breathed evenly, then opened his eyes once the threat of moisture overwhelming them receded. As he looked up the golden yellow drapes around him, he admired the work that had gone into their pattern, creating the effect of cascading leaves of a willow tree. They were beautiful, but as he stared up at them he could not help but think they were weeping for him. Life was cruel: he had worked so hard, fought tirelessly, ignored the prejudice from those who were against raising anyone up from the lower ranks, and tried to be hero enough for his Sophia — yet right now he was laid abed, broken with the cold threat of her father's words echoing in his head. It hurt; they all did: his leg, his heart, and the memories that he did not wish to see anymore when he closed his eyes as the canons sounded and men screamed.

'We have sent for the doctor, Lieutenant.' Cynthia's soft voice drifted into his thoughts and he glanced into her caring eyes. She had a delicate and concerned face.

'Sorry, I drifted off for a moment, lost in thought. Thank you for your kindness.' He saw her features relax, as she obviously thought he had slipped off into deeper oblivion.

'I will ask Judd to see to your . . . to make you comfortable and change you into . . . so the doctor will be able to look at . . . ' Cynthia nodded as if she had expressed her meaning eloquently.

The poor woman was all a fluster, he thought.

'Judd!' The man was only a step behind her, and when he responded with a 'Yes, ma'am,' she nearly leapt to the side of the bed. Quickly regaining her composure, she ordered him to make sure the lieutenant was made comfortable and change him and so on as needed. She nodded at James and quickly left them together.

'Where did she come from?' James asked as Judd sat down on the bed next to him, obviously amused; and James realised he had deliberately made her jump.

'Well, Lieutenant, hero, martyr . . . ' Judd began.

'I am not dead yet, Rob,' James replied to his old friend.

'You will be, my man, if you dare touch Miss Sophia again.' Judd's face was full of mischief as he raised both eyebrows at James.

'I know that.'

'Good, because you have managed to leave with a boot behind your backside, and yet here you are all cosy in the Willow guest room. You have risen far, but not high enough for Miss Sophia. Now, to answer your question, that lady has been here for nearly four years and is a breath of fresh air. Sir went to London and came back with a wife.

Miss Sophia likes her, but she is as light as a feather in character. Good, though. I'll not see her wronged. We all feel protective of her because she brings this mausoleum to life. Now let's get you changed and see if you are a wounded soldier or an amputee-to-be.' He stood up and faced James, ready to remove the boots first.

'Rob, don't ever say that!' James snapped.

Rob nodded. 'Sorry, man. Guess I'm just a little jealous. Here's me running around passages and serving the great and the good, and you are out there being feasted as a hero.' Rob shrugged and very carefully pulled off James' boot.

James nearly screamed in pain as it was removed from his injured leg. Once his breeches had been removed, it was clear to see that the bruising and swelling needed attention. James was relieved that all was healthy.

'Guess you have earned it,' Rob said as he continued to remove James' uniform and give him a wash-down before slipping a nightshirt over him. James had two scars on his back where he had nearly been cut down by a sabre. They were old and healed. 'What sights you must have seen, James, and all for the love of a woman.'

'A wonderful woman, who I still love,' James confessed to his old friend. 'Besides, it felt good to do something where I felt needed and had some skill at it.'

'Then you are a doomed man, if not by Sir then by your stupid feelings of honour that may take you rejected and broken-hearted back to the fray,' Rob replied, shaking his head as he picked up the uniform. 'I'll have these cleaned.'

'Rob, find out what you can about this Huntley chap. If he is being considered for Sophia, perhaps there is hope if we can discredit him?' James asked.

'You always were a dreamer. I'll do what we servants do best, sir: listen silently as we blend in with the furniture.' He laughed. 'Remember to call her Miss Sophia at all times.'

'Very good; you may go,' James said, and saw Rob bundle his shirt up as if he was going to hurl it at him. But when the door opened and a young maid appeared with a hot drink for James, Rob left with a polite bow.

★   ★   ★

Sophia greeted the doctor as soon as he stepped out of the carriage the next morning. She was quick to tell him where James was and explain his situation, having first spoken to Judd and the maid since they alone had been in the room. When Sir Kenneth strode out of his study, she stepped back and watched the men ascend the great staircase, deep in conversation.

She felt Cynthia's fingers slip around hers, and looked at her.

'Do not worry. Doctor Aimes is a man who has many years of experience.

He'll see the lieutenant is well.' She squeezed Sophia's hand gently, and Sophia acknowledged the kindly gesture.

Cynthia was sweet. She never wished anyone harm. But if she knew how Sophia's heart ached at that moment to be there for her James, she would let her run up the stairs and follow. 'We must wait in the morning room. Your father will join us there. We cannot do more, dear Sophia,' her voice whispered into her ear and she gently led Sophia away.

'I am just concerned. He is so young and I hope the leg has not gone bad,' Sophia explained.

'I can see you are concerned for him, Sophia. Perhaps you should not let your father see that, though. I wouldn't want him to think that it was more than just concern.' Cynthia's words made Sophia look directly at her innocent face. She scrunched up her nose and then winked at her. 'We must be a little more discreet if you wish to be allowed to even talk with the young man.'

'Why ever would I wish to do that?' Sophia remarked defensively.

'Because he is your dear friend. But whatever he was to you, if he is to be that again, you are going to have to be careful. You take my advice. When a man's heart is set, he will do anything to get what he wants. You must protect your lieutenant from open folly. But when a woman wants something against a man's will, then you have to take the time to figure out how best to allow them to change their will to yours. It is not easy, but it can be done.' She sat next to Sophia on the sofa by the fire with a very self-assured expression upon her innocent face.

'Why, Cynthia, you give excellent and worldly advice,' Sophia said, admiring the thinking that went on behind her seemingly shallow persona.

'Of course. I have lived in this world longer than you and have survived a father who died all too soon, plus I had a mother who remarried badly and a brother who inherited and would have gambled our fortune away. My dear Kenneth is a man I love and admire beyond the stars, but he knows how ill fortune nearly destroyed me.' She placed her hands in her lap and looked content with her life, and yet the words she shared spoke of her near ruin.

'So how did you come to bring so much affluence to our own fortunes?' Sophia was amazed by this revelation.

'Why, it was a simple solution once I found the right man, and your father was that because he is above all else fair and honest. I got him to gamble with my brother, knowing that Kenneth would win easily. He lost the family fortune on a bet to your father, and me into the bargain. If it was not for Kenneth's generous spirit, dear Simeon would be languishing in Newgate Prison as a debtor. Instead, he is in Edinburgh learning medicine. If he fails to keep up his studies, Kenneth will disown him. I believe he has made him a better man.'

'Why tell me all this now, Cynthia?' Sophia asked.

'Because you should know. I have wanted to explain all to you for long enough, but it takes time to truly know and grow to love someone you can trust.'

Sophia had naively never realised that, whilst she was feeling magnanimous because she had accepted Cynthia, her step-mother was going through a similar emotional acceptance of her. It made her feel quite arrogant and humbled.

'You think you love James, but Lucas is very handsome and attentive. Before your future is determined by men, know your own mind. They will both be here for a while. So we shall see who wins or deserves your affections, or if either fails to measure up.' She laughed at Sophia's shocked expression but, as a man's scream was heard echoing down the stairs, both women's faces stared at the open door as they waited for news of James' plight.

6

'Ladies, I am sorry I took so long returning yesterday that I missed your presence again.' He smiled apologetically and then asked Sophia, 'What news of our wounded hero?' Lucas returned to greet the ladies, having been told by Brent that the situation with James had required some operation and that Sir Kenneth would be with them all shortly.

Sophia shook her head. 'We await Father to come back down. They have been up there for hours,' she said, trying to keep an even voice as the growing distress within her seemed overbearing. She knew soiled cloths had been brought down, and fresh water and dressings taken back up by Judd and the maid. It was all too reminiscent of that day when, as a child, her life had changed from pampered daughter with a doting mother to one of loneliness.

'Thank goodness you have returned to us safely, Mr Huntley,' Cynthia said.

'Yes; the hour was later than I had hoped, for I had to take the journey more slowly because of my horse's injured fetlock. It seems that the day was one for injuries. The gamekeeper, I am informed, is very good at healing horses of their ailments, so I have left him with your man. Meanwhile, our man upstairs seems to be having a hard time. I do hope it can be saved.'

'What can be?' Sophia felt her head lighten. What was he saying?

'His leg, my dear Miss Sophia, not his life. He is young and strong and so should survive this ordeal. Yet he may have to face the future as a cripple, I'm afraid, as so many of our wounded heroes do.' He dipped his head as if it was a harsh but unstated truth which needed vocalising.

Cynthia let out a gasp and swooned slightly, which broke the intensity of the moment and gave Sophia a chance to regain her own composure as she went to find Cynthia's smelling salts. They were kept in a cabinet by the door in case she had one of her infrequent turns of nerves.

'My apologies,' Huntley said straight away as if he realised his comments were perhaps too graphic for her delicate countenance.

'Poor boy,' Cynthia whispered as she sat up straight again and shot Sophia a quick warning glance.

'We should be prayerful and hopeful that this is not the case,' Sophia said; her demeanour was covering up the inner turmoil that had threatened to undo her moments earlier.

'Of course, of course,' Lucas agreed. 'We should always pray and wish for the best. I am certain that the doctor's skills will be better than any who serve in the field. I wonder where he was when he was injured and treated.' He looked at Sophia, who shrugged.

Why was he labouring this point? Did he want to see her cry? Was it some sort of test of the depth of affection she had still for James? No, of course not. This man did not know that the two had ever met before. Sophia realised that her anxiety was leading her mind astray.

'I shall order hot chocolate for us all. Would that be suitable for you, Mr Huntley?' She forced a polite smile. 'I find it very calming.'

'Yes, yes, dear lady, of course. It would be just the thing. I left a bag in the hall,' he said, and took a step after Sophia.

'Lucas.' Cynthia patted the sofa next to her where Sophia had been sitting. 'Sophia will see it is taken to your room. Come and keep me company whilst we wait for news. Mr Huntley, warm yourself by the fire whilst Sophia organises the servants for me. She is so good at it. In fact, dear Sophia is gifted in whatever she turns her hand to.' Cynthia smiled sweetly.

★　★　★

'What have you done?' James asked after Judd and Brent released his torso. A board had been placed under his limb, and secured by ankles tethers, so that his body was rigid and could not lash out as the doctor worked his ways.

He had been plied with an opiate — laudanum, he suspected, but even so, the pain had passed through the haze, bringing him back to consciousness. He remembered hearing screaming; he knew the sound had escaped his own lips. At first it seemed like it was from a source above him, but then he had owned it. His vision was not as clear as it should be, but he could not see masses of blood-stained bedding or bloody saws. The doctor was replacing his jacket and did not look like he had butchered a pig, so some hope returned that he had survived the ordeal intact.

James inched his hand slowly down his right thigh. As far as he could reach, he still had a leg, but he could not feel if his foot was cold, numb or missing. He did not want to cry; he had been selected for the forlorn hope twice, surviving being the first through the breach on both occasions with only minor injuries, and then had never wavered. Yet now he felt that he could weep like a child.

'Fortunately for you, Dr Aimes served on HMS *Royal Sovereign*, under Admiral Collingwood at Trafalgar no less. Two heroes grace my house this day,' Sir Kenneth said with genuine pride.

'Please, Sir Kenneth, you are too kind.' The doctor seemed to like the praise all the same.

'No, I tell it as it is, Archibald. As I was saying, he was there at Trafalgar and was proud to save many a limb. Despite stooping to participating as a surgeon, he learned a great deal from the experience — didn't you, Archibald?' Sir Kenneth asked his friend.

The use of the word 'surgeon' only served to scare James further.

'Indeed, indeed,' Dr Aimes agreed. 'Sometimes from the horror of war, new progress is made through need and circumstance.'

'My leg, though — it is there? What of my leg, sir?' James' voice sounded slurred, even to his own ears, and very quiet.

'I am afraid that I had to break the fracture again. It had not set right at all. Perhaps in haste they splinted it, but had not time to straighten it accurately. I also had to open up part of the shin to release the bad humours, but it is all good now. You must not be moved for a week or two, and then mobility will be slow until you can use your limb with a splint and walking sticks. Then it will be a gradual recovery. But, with good luck and nursing, and with no infection, you could be looking at walking without a stick in three months and riding again in six. The key is not to rush at the recovery, and then all should go well.' The doctor was smiling, but James stared blankly at him and then at the face of Sir Kenneth. He could not read the man's thoughts.

'Perhaps I could use my old accommodation, sir, until I can move freely,' he said, and saw the looks exchanged by Brent and Judd. Their thoughts were easier to interpret. They did not think that a good idea, but what else could he say?

'Wouldn't hear of it, James. You will look upon this as your room until you are well enough to walk out of it on your own feet, unheeded. Then we will talk of what you should do next.' Sir Kenneth patted him on the shoulder. 'Rest easy. You have a benefactor who will see you well again.' His face was still emotionless.

James could only feel gratitude, for he had nowhere else to go and was hardly in a position to leave even if he did.

'Archibald, thank you, my dear friend. You have done a great service in more ways than you know. Join me for a brandy?' Sir Kenneth said as they left the room with his friend and Brent following behind.

Judd hung back. 'You jammy sod, Jimmy my boy,' he said.

'Rob, I thought he'd sawed it off.

God, I nearly fell to pieces at the thought,' James blurted out, eyes filled with relief.

'You may be a hero, man, but you are still human and allowed to scream. I would certainly have. The knock he gave that leg bone to split it again . . . Mind, he was right; it would have come through the skin if it had been left. Reminded me of old Thunder — remember when he had to be put out of his misery when he fell badly?' Judd shook his head.

'Rob, please. Time and place.' James had known this man since they were both boys serving in the stables doing all the hard graft of mucking and sweeping out, grooming, polishing — anything until they were taught how to ride, train and become at one with the animals they tended and cared for. He had missed him a great deal when he was sent away. Rob knew the truth of his association with Sophia, as he had acted as lookout for them on many an occasion.

'Sorry, Jimmy. Just saying . . . ' Rob laughed.

'Please ask Mrs Gribbins what she can do to ensure it does not turn bad,' James pleaded.

'You dote, you don't still believe in old Gribbins' remedies. God in heaven, man! The doctor has left medication and clear instructions. He uses a new brown liquid that is supposed to stop the badness settling in. So when you see them stitches, that yellowy colour is not you going off but the ointment stuff. You, it appears, are being looked after. Why, I know not; but do nothing other than what you are told to do. Being turned out at the moment would be your death knell.

7

Two days later, Sophia had not been anywhere near James. Cynthia had acted as a chaperone with her and Lucas Huntley when he was not engrossed in conversation with her father. He was being very attentive. Sophia tried not to look at him in the same way she considered James, but he was attractive and listened when she gave an opinion on anything. Unusually for a man, he frequently asked for her thoughts on anything from estate matters to the country and even, on occasion, the reports of the wars.

'Where is Father, Cynthia?' she asked as Sophia found her in the orangery on her chaise longue, happily basking in the warmth of the day and sipping lemon water.

'He has taken Lucas to the races. I am not expecting them back before

Thursday.' She did not open her eyes. 'Two whole days to do . . . nothing in . . . how absolute bliss can be.'

'Then you enjoy your peace,' Sophia said and left her, going straight up the stairs. She had a book in her hand as she had intended to join Cynthia and read a while, expecting Huntley to be hovering near her; but this was her chance. She entered James' bedchamber through the small room next to it. It was the bathing room where servants would enter through a hidden door with warm water and fresh towels. Opening the door slightly, she saw James sitting up in the bed staring out of the window.

'Whoever you are, please enter and save me from a slow and painful death by boredom.' He did not even look around.

'Well we cannot have that, can we?' Sophia said, and watched his head almost spin around like an owl. However, he was not sighting his prey, but was staring at her with grateful eyes, if not ones that betrayed his desire.

'Oh Sophia!' He tried to change position. Instantly she ran to his bedside and sat carefully on the edge of it, holding his shoulders gently to make him sit back. She felt the solid strength of his muscles and realised how much he had changed since she hugged that nervous youth of yesteryear. 'You should not be in here!'

His eyes were moist, his colour slightly high.

'Do you have a fever, James?' she asked.

'Not the type that Dr Aimes could cure. Sophia, we are undone. I will die if I am sent away from here in this condition. My leg has to be saved if I am to be any good to anyone — to you. You should not risk coming here . . . if your father should see you . . . '

'Oh James, you have not forgotten me. I was so scared you would be hurt or killed or worse, fall in love with a beautiful woman in some exotic land. Father is away for a few days with Mr Huntley. Do not worry.' She stroked the back of his hand gently.

He laughed. 'Oh Sophia, you would have me dead rather than forget you.' He shook his head. 'Are those the words of love?' He lifted his arm up and stroked her shoulder with his hand as she gently leaned forward and rested on his chest, giving him a controlled but sensitive hug.

'What else? Tell me if I hurt you, James,' Sophia said, lifting her head so that their faces were only an inch apart. She kissed moist, ready and willing lips. Moments of bliss passed by, but not as Cynthia was experiencing, reclined in the orangery; here, wrapped in his arms, the emotions inside her were overwhelming, heady and delightful. When finally they parted, they stared at each other as if they had just begun their friendship again exactly at the point where fate had made them separate years earlier. Yet she was a woman full grown and he a man of the world.

'What are we to do?' she asked.

'Be patient. Find a way. You and I are

soul-mates. We should be forever joined, always meant to be together.'

'Yes, it is true. But Father has Lucas Huntley in his sights for me, I am sure. He wants you to be well and does not hold a grudge. But he will not bless our marriage, James, and that breaks my heart, for I do not wish to break his.' Sophia sat up. 'It appears we face an insurmountable problem, but we will somehow overcome this.'

'You and I will be together, but this you must not risk until I may convalesce in the basket chair like an old man, seated in the orangery or garden. Then, where we may be watched, you can read to or entertain me with your enlightening and witty conversation. But until I can support my own weight, I cannot support you.' James' lips clenched.

'How will we win Father over, James?' She looked beseechingly into his eyes.

'There is a way, but it will take time and a trip to London. Until then, you and I will have to be above reproach. We need his trust first, and then his love will follow,' James said. His words were smothered as Sophia caressed him again. The ache in both of them became too much, and she stood up suddenly.

'You are quite correct, as you were back then. It was my eagerness that brought us low, and it will be your strength and honour that will raise us high. I will do as you say, but I am worried that arrangements for a match with Mr Huntley may be underway as we speak. Have we the time to make this happen?' She swallowed, as she could read his expression of concern.

'You must slow things down with their plans. Once he has set off to London, then time will be our own again. I do not know this man. Tell me what you have learned of him?' James asked, and inched himself up the bed a little so he was more upright. His forehead creased with pain as he flinched at the effort.

Sophia explained about the business that he and his father would be setting up in the New World in New South

Wales. When she saw the change in James' face, she stopped talking.

'What is it?' she asked. 'Do you know Mr Lucas Huntley Senior?'

'Can you fetch me pen and paper? And please be discreet. I need you to act as my accomplice in this. Until I have a reply, no one must know that I have sent this letter. I do not wish to be questioned upon it.' James was holding her hand tightly.

'Why? What is the urgency?' Sophia asked.

'Do you not see, my dear Sophia? If this man's fortune and future lie in Australia, then any wife he takes will be at his side. I would lose you forever, as their plans may be hurried.'

A single tear escaped Sophia's eyes as she saw the distress this revelation caused in him. His words, so obvious and yet so stupidly overlooked by her, stung deeply. To leave England, leave James when he had just found her again, and to abandon her father forever was almost too much to bear.

Even the thought of never hearing Cynthia's girlish and impish laugh made her want to sob.

'Daisy, check that the lieutenant is comfortable.' Brent's voice resounded down the corridor outside.

Sophia ran to the other room without further words being spoken, but her mind was filled with them. Would her father really sanction this match with Huntley? Was Cynthia sufficient family for him to live contentedly in England? Surely not!

8

'Tell me you are not a spectre or my erstwhile past come to haunt me,' James whispered as he felt a warm hand slip beneath the bed covers and slide across his chest. Sophia did not have to say a word. He knew her perfume; could feel the tickle of a wayward hair as she slipped inside the coverlet and hugged him. Oh how he ached, more than the leg that throbbed or itched in turn, but in his heart and in part of his being that he longed for her to touch . . . but then again not, as he could only lay still abed. One more week already had gone by very slowly except for the visits from his dear Sophia, who was no more able to stay away from him when the opportunity presented itself than he could send her away. He had strict instructions not to twist, turn or attempt to sit up.

'You must leave me, you wanton woman,' he whispered, and felt her breasts move against his side as she stifled a giggle. Goodness, he realised there was only the thickness of cloth of his night shirt and her nightdress between them. She did not speak, which made him wonder what she was going to do next. She was being very brave or foolish. Lucas had returned, as had Sir Kenneth; but within a day they had returned to York for yet another appointment. He had found this out from Judd.

When her fingers slowly traced his chest down to his navel, where they lingered but showed no sign of going lower, he felt a curl touch his cheek and knew something was very wrong. The faint perfume he had thought he knew was no more than the delicate smell of orange blossom. He grabbed the hand before it could reach his manhood and snapped his words out, 'Who are you?'

The chuckle was unmistakable, although it was subdued. Cynthia sat up beside him. He released her hand as soon as he realised who had broken his sleep in such a brazen way. He felt for the table at the side of his bed and was about to try and pull himself up when she lightly jumped off the bed and walked around to his side.

'Please forgive me, Lieutenant,' Cynthia whispered, and put his hand back by his side. 'Do not distress yourself so. I merely wanted to know if Sophia behaved improperly with you and if you would, given the opportunity, betray her.'

'You play dangerous games, lady,' he admonished, then dared to add, 'Are you not ashamed to stoop so low?'

She placed a hand over her mouth as if she would laugh out loud. Then, regaining her composure, she let her hands drop in front of her. Her silhouette was blurred as the room was so dusky. 'Dear James, I had no intention of going any further. I merely wanted to know if the soldier had honour, or was more base an animal in nature rather than a gentleman in his intent. You see, I am a married woman and understand these things, while Sophia does not. You passed the test. But I know you will not divulge my direct approach to your love, or my Kenneth, as it would not be in either of our interests. However, I would say this — you have to up your game, James. Kenneth is increasingly impressed by Huntley Junior. Time is ticking, and if you want our lovely Sophia to say goodbye to her home and country for good, you will have to act swiftly.'

'You say this, ma'am, but how am I to act at all? I am not allowed to even sit in that infernal old man's basket chair until two more days have passed.'

'Dear boy, tomorrow I am going to town to collect my dresses and essentials for the coming season and will be taking with me the two upper housemaids. Brent has to go to meet his master in town, and that will leave Sophia in charge of the house and you. She yearns for you. Be daring, be bold, ask her to touch you gently. You are in bed. I know she visits you to 'read', so make a move. Huntley has a way of making her laugh, but I see a wolf not a sheep.'

'What if I scare her off? She is a lady and I am a . . . '

'You are a hero! You were in her eyes when you were younger, and you must be one for real again. Now, to speed things up, I will go and collect the post — it should have arrived from London by now — and see if you have a reply to the letter you had posted upon your arrival.'

'How would you know that, when Sophia sent it down for me?' James realised he had greatly underestimated this lady, as had Sophia and Rob too.

'My dear boy, you would be surprised what I know. It pays to be observant and yet unobserved. Now, tell Cynthia what it is you are up to and I promise that I will help you.'

'Why?' asked James, his head full of suspicions.

'Because I have no wish to see

Sophia leave this Hall, let alone the country, and there is plenty of room on this estate for you two to have a happy home. But I will know the truth of it, or you will be sent away, far away. I love Sophia as a sister; we are too near in age to be mama and daughter. But I will not have my bliss here ruined by anyone.' She patted him on the shoulder and pulled a chair over and sat by the bed. 'So, Lieutenant James Dalesman, tell me all.'

★　★　★

Sophia returned to her bedchamber, her hands shaking as she balled them into fists. She had spent an hour making herself as presentable and alluring as she could in her new nightgown. She had bathed and perfumed herself in the eau de toilette of the citrus fruits and washed and dried her hair, letting it cascade around her shoulders. With her woven silk shawl draped around her shoulders, she had tiptoed along the upper corridor to slip into her lover's bed. He may well be incapacitated, but he knew how to please her and she him. So the image of Cynthia slipping into his room had shocked her. The woman had no shawl, just her nightdress. James had not called out.

She had gone to follow, but she could not hear a sound from within, and then the undistinguishable sound of stifled giggles. She made out his voice, spoken low and then only mutterings. If she burst in, there would be a scene, and the whole house would know what had happened. James would be injured and thrown out. Cynthia would break her father's heart, and she would be forever imprisoned in the Hall as his keeper. This moment of folly on Cynthia's part would ruin everything forever. She would wait in the shadows, and when the brazen wench reappeared, Sophia would grab her arm and take her to her room where she could explain her actions.

But . . . Sophia waited . . . Cynthia

did not reappear, and like her heart, Sophia grew cold and tired of waiting. She would face them tomorrow, each in turn, and see if either had anything to say to her. If they kept this secret, then so would she. Lucas Huntley could take her to the New World, because her old one would be forever broken. She went to her bed and stared into blackness, for sleep would not come.

9

If Sophia had been a man, she would be able to ride away and leave all of her problems behind her on a whim, But she was a woman, and that irked her more now than at any other frustrating time in her life.

The next morning, after little and fitful sleep, she met Cynthia entering the morning room as she was leaving. Here they normally shared a pleasant, if not entertaining, chat before beginning their day. Today, Sophia had broken her fast early and was about to leave. She had hoped to miss her completely and be able to speak to James before looking at her. How could the woman behave so brazenly as to slip into a stranger's bedchamber when her husband was away on business? She almost laughed at her own stupidity. No woman would consider doing it when he was in the Hall, would she? But why pick James, an invalid, someone who could not protest or walk away? Someone who loved her step-daughter.

Perhaps that was the very reason she had. She wanted to tease him — a sordid game that appealed to her girlish sense of fun.

'Morning, Sophia. Isn't the sun beautiful this morning? We should go for a walk around the gardens today and . . . ' She stopped talking and looked at the table where Sophia's plate was already being cleared away, and then she glanced back at Sophia and the door as if realising that she had been about to leave.

'Yes, it is. I thought I might go for a morning ride,' Sophia said, knowing that Cynthia hated the notion of riding any time of the day. She could abide carriage rides and the occasional short trip on a gig, but never did Cynthia trust her own life to the whim of a horse to carry her safely.

'Well, you take care and enjoy

yourself, but no reckless jumping. That is not safe or ladylike. I thought you would be spending time with the young lieutenant. Your father will return this evening, and — '

'He will mend more quickly if he rests undisturbed, I am sure,' Sophia interrupted, and walked to the doorway. 'Enjoy your breakfast,' she added as she was about to step away.

'Sophia!' Cynthia called with a sharpish note to her normally friendly voice.

'Yes, Cynthia, was there something you wanted to say?'

'Yes; you are not wearing a riding outfit, dear,' Her lips smiled, but her eyes did not.

'I was just going to change. I had only just decided to go out. Was that all?' Sophia asked innocently, or so she thought, but her eyes betrayed her anger and hurt.

'Yes, dear, but be sure you do not fall. We do not want two injured souls lying ill abed with damaged limbs. I shall be going to town today,' Cynthia added. 'You will be quite alone in the house, as the servants are all busy elsewhere.' She tilted her head mischievously on one side and smiled impishly back at her.

'No, I am sure we do not.' Sophia ran up the stairs and almost flew into her room to quickly change into her riding outfit. Once James' morning tray had been removed, she entered his room.

'Enjoy your ride.'

Closing the door behind her to James' room, she held her riding crop in her hand. Looking at his tired, pale face, she wondered if it was lack of sleep or the effect of being imprisoned in a bed for nigh on ten days that had caused his complexion to pale. So she opened two of the windows slightly, and instantly air rushed into the stuffy room. She drew back the drapes, and light flooded in along with a warm summer breeze.

He looked at the crop hanging from a wrist strap on her arm and pointed at it. 'Now, you would not hit a man when he was already down, would you?' James asked, and half smiled at her. 'However, if I am to be allowed up tomorrow for only a few hours, it will be a start, but we must take care not to be seen to be too familiar in each other's company.' He appeared to be genuinely concerned.

'No, that we must never do.' Sophia's voice sounded cold even to her own ears.

James stared at her in disbelief. 'What is wrong, Sophia? Has your father returned early with news? Are you to wed the Huntley man already? Has an arrangement or announcement been made?'

'No, he is away all of the day with Father as usual,' she said in her normal voice; but her heart felt sad.

James patted the bed next to him. 'Then stay a while,' he said, but was obviously surprised when she did not move.

'Is there something you would like to

say or tell me, James?' she asked. Sophia could feel the emotions welling up within her and clamped her lips firmly together to try and stop from blubbering like a small child. Her greatest dream had almost been realised, and here before her lay the man she had adored for five years who she had longed for, yet her stepmother had entered this very room with a liaison in the night.

What was she to think?

'Sit down, Sophia. Do not be upset with me. Tell me all and I shall try and explain if there is something amiss.'

'You are here . . . You are here in my home,' she began, but her words were failing her, for to say what she wanted to would incriminate Cynthia and could destroy her family — it was James who must trust her with the truth.

'Yes, is that not joyous?' He reached out his hand to her.

'I would have thought so, and I would have thought that this turn of events would have been enough for you

. . . that I would have been enough for you. That is, if we could ever be truly with each other.' She tried to hold back the rush of emotions that threatened to be released by her words.

James flopped back and looked up at the weeping willow leaves.

'They weep for me, Sophia. Just as I weep for us. You are more than I deserve, and I could never want a woman more. I have not lived in a stable block these last five years, Sophia; I have seen the world, life and death and all the horror and beauty in between. I have had you in my heart through battle and peace, through long marches and sieges. Yet here I am, trapped by my own body. How could I have wronged you and risked your ire? I wish to be with you for the rest of my life.'

'How indeed? You tell me.' Sophia did not move. 'Your words are well spoken, your sincerity touching; so tell me how could it even be possible that you would be able to play me false?'

'You think I would betray our love? Is

that how much you hold me in trust in your heart?' He raised his eyebrows.

Sophia could not understand how he was batting her questions back at her instead of unravelling the secrets of the previous night. Was he playing a game with her? 'Yesterday I would have said that you were beyond reproach. I would never have doubted you.' She raised her eyebrows back at him.

'So why has that changed overnight?' he asked.

Sophia watched his features quiver slightly when he mentioned the word night. He nodded slowly. 'Did you chance to come here under the cover of darkness, Sophia? Would you be so bold?'

'And what if I did?' she asked, knowing that the truth of it was finally revealed.

'Then today you might stand there, crop in hand and accuse an innocent man of a wrongdoing he did not and would never commit.' James folded his arms across his chest. 'Not guilty of anything, milord,' he said.

'Then what explanation would you give?' Sophia breathed deeply. 'Do not treat this as a joke, James. Please do not. I would know the truth.'

'Just believe me when I say that nothing happened that was of any import.' James looked beyond her.

A voice from behind her answered. 'He wouldn't,' Cynthia offered, 'because he is an honourable man, and you would place him in a situation where even if the truth were told, it would discredit another lady, for it was I who came to him!' She snapped her words out and shut the door behind her. She was dressed in her day coat, ready to leave on her journey to Gorebeck. 'I have not time to explain now, but trust us both, dear sweet Sophia. For as guilty as I am for putting a daring test before your young man, you are more guilty, for you would have broken your word to your father and done more than an unmarried single lady should do. So put that crop away, for I am sorely tempted to use it on you for your highhandedness this morning with me.'

'I . . . '

'Hush, child. I have a mission to complete and a journey to make. Stay with your man and never judge me ill again!' She nodded to James. 'I will be back before my husband returns this evening. Be here and put that petulant lip away!' Cynthia swung around and flounced out of the room, slamming the door shut behind her.

'How dare she?' Sophia said. 'This is my home and you are my father's guest!'

'Simply because she knows she did something wrong, but it was for the best of reasons. However, I need to explain, so please put down your crop, as I cannot defend myself and you are frightening me where many a Hussar has failed.'

She saw the glint in his eyes and dropped the crop on the chair, unpinning her hat and placed it there also.

'I need to know the truth,' Sophia said.

'Yes, you keep demanding it. Very well,

then be seated. For it is this. She wanted to know if I played you false or would take advantage of you. I did neither, so I passed her stupid test. However, she knows about my letter, and that is why I have had to trust her. This is where I owe you an apology; for, Sophia, there is more to my story that I have not had the opportunity to share with you.'

'Then tell me now, for I am still angry with her. Her behaviour has been more like that of a courtesan than a respectable wife.' Sophia felt vexed with Cynthia and hoped that her father's heart was safe in the woman's keeping, because she had certainly captured it. There was no fool like an old one, she thought — but in her case a young one, it would appear.

'I have wealth coming to me,' James said.

'How so?' she asked, surprised by this revelation.

'I was fortunate enough to fall upon some trinkets whilst on reconnaissance. Soldiers often acquire what has been passed over, or discarded by the enemy. I was very lucky to see something being buried by a Frenchman who could not carry it anymore. He obviously intended to return when the war was over. When he left, I unearthed his treasure. It has been converted into pounds, and I await the documents to prove that I have these funds available to me from the bankers in Threadneedle St, London.'

'Should this not have been put towards the war effort?' she asked naively.

'No! For it was not taken from a specific place where we were invading. There was no way of knowing who the man was or why he would leave valuables in a hole in the ground. If he were so careless with it, then who am I to question my good fortune in discovering it? Believe me, it is legitimately mine, but I will only have proof it exists at all once I have the letter.'

'What of its owner?' she asked.

'He is long gone, and he was a Frenchman who no doubt stole it from a Spaniard. This is war, Sophia. It is as much mine as the Hall is your father's.' His colour was high.

He obviously could not understand why she questioned him and instead was not rubbing her hands in glee.

'But Father's was inherited and has been in the family for generations,' Sophia protested, as she did not want to think of her future being the result of a theft.

'Sophia, how many slaves' lives went into providing your family's wealth? So please do not judge me for keeping what the good Lord showed me was there for the taking. That with my rank and recommendation must surely put me in a different light with your father?' He was sitting forward as if pleading for her to accept his reasoning.

Sophia stood up grabbed her hat and crop and ran through the house to the stables, his words ringing in her ears, the truth in them hard to bear, but bear them she must. For what had been said could never be unsaid. Yet, she must return calmed after a hard ride and act to all as if none of this had happened. Her future was looking bright only the day before, but now whichever way she looked it was tainted. The delightful Cynthia was dangerous and calculating. Jeremy Huntley wanted her wealth and her, she had no doubt of that; but he would take her to a foreign world. Her father was completely blind to his wife's character, and James ... He held hidden grudges because of her wealth — did he see her as the produce of blood money?

She had never questioned where her family's wealth was from, presuming the sheep provided the upkeep along with the tenants' tithes. How stupid. Of course there was not enough to be gained from that to pay for horses, stabling, parties and their way of life. He was right. James was so right! Her whole world was built on a vile trade and the corruption of men. How her heart ached for a simpler life. She rode to the hillock and looked back at the grand Hall, her home. Only three of them lived there, and a dozen or more servants. She did not even know how many tended the estate. Why had she never questioned any of it, but just accepted, as her father had said many a time, that some were born to toil others, to lead? She led the household and the estate. But they provided a good living for their servants and tenants. Many depended on them.

She could not change the world, but she would change her life. She realised that Cynthia was quite capable of running the house, but why should she bother as long as Sophia was there to do all the tedious parts of her role? She turned her horse back and rode towards the stables.

'I am no child!' she said as she galloped back. Cynthia could have her world and Sophia would determine her own. It would have James in it, but as a woman in her own right, not as his prize.

10

Sophia returned to the Hall, changed and went to James' room with a gift of three books selected from the library. One was written about the Isle of Wight, the next was a collection of papers and drawings on anatomy from Michelangelo, Leonardo Da Vinci to Charles Bell's more recent paper on anatomy and art, and the third was a book of instruction in the running of an estate.

'Here, James, you may fill your hours in useful pursuit,' she said without sitting down, placing the books on his lap.

'Does this mean I am forgiven my outburst?' he said coyly.

'You said what you thought, and I have reflected upon your words. There may be some truth in them, but I am hardly going to apologize for the way of the world and my benefit from it, for I was born into this family. Change is coming. There are protests, and parliament will debate. This is not in our control, but you should read these and then your understanding may well improve. Put fear of your body's weaknesses aside as you understand it more and strengthen your mind as well. Look to how to look after your surroundings and invest in the land and make your own self-sufficient estate; or if he is willing to allow you, then help Father with this one, if you can separate your conscience from the past that our ignorant forefathers were involved in. For Father has no connection with the trade now — I know this because he supports the reformers, such as Mr Wilberforce.' Having delivered her words in what she thought was an eloquent fashion, she was content.

James nodded his approval. 'And this one?' he said, seemingly quite stunned by her deliverance as he raised the small travel book on the Isle of Wight.

'Seeing as we will not be able to do a tour of Europe when we are wed, and I have no intention of going to Scotland as it is too far, the roads horrendous I have heard, and very cold, so I wish to go somewhere southern and warmer. We shall honeymoon on the Isle of Wight, Ventnor perhaps or Shanklin.'

He laughed. 'Sophia, you have sorted all this out in a few angry hours. So now you have made your point, and before I am given a copy of *A Vindication of the Rights of Women* or some other testament to the importance of women and their need for separate legal rights from men, can I speak to you?'

Sophia nodded, warmed at the fact he had realised the one topic she had not given him reading matter on was in fact the works of Mary Wollstonecraft because she was still reading that particular one, much to her father's chagrin.

'I am sorry. I should have told you straight away that Cynthia was not so innocent or light of wit as you and Rob appeared to think she was . . . ' He put his tongue in his cheek for a moment as her eyes widened when he mentioned Rob.

He had included the thoughts of a servant on a person of the house, which meant he had gossiped with them, which was something that showed up his lack of class and understanding of his position.

'I know what you are thinking, Sophia, so do not send me back to the stables with my ignorant head in my hands. Rob is a servant, but we were friends back then and we are still now. I had the same problem in the army, for once you are raised from the ranks you have to carve out a new role; you are not one of the men but must order them and have their trust and acceptance. Otherwise, they will think you have stepped above your place and will bring you down. Yet I was also prejudiced by the rich and pampered officers of a certain 'class'. Yes, I felt resentful and my comments were meant to lash out and hurt you about the origins of this family's wealth. I apologise for that too; it was beneath me and undeserved by you. Your father is a good man and one who I am grateful to a thousand times over.' He sighed.

'Your apologies are accepted, but be careful what you tell Rob. He may not be as trustworthy as you think, and could use his new source of information to gain attention below stairs. Brent hates that kind of thing.'

'Sophia, think a minute. Who is it that knows the world below stairs better? Would it be you or me?'

She sniffed. There was no answer to that and he knew it.

'My family does not exist anymore. You, Mrs Gribbins — whom I have yet to greet — and Rob are as dear to me as my own father was. How can I act superior?' He shook his head. 'I cannot in my heart, for I know I am not their better, just more fortunate.'

'Then do not act anything. Be yourself and stop apologising for it. You have changed; for how easily you ate at our table, kept conversation, and used all the correct cutlery.'

He smiled. 'I suppose I have.'

'Now, you can tell me what she did to you — no matter how base! I am not a child anymore, and I would know what dear Cynthia is capable of. If she has played me for a fool, then I need to be more aware.'

James stared at her for a moment and Sophia's heart sank, for instantly she realised there was more to tell. He had obviously thought their discussion had averted her from the topic of the previous night.

'Sophia, she is collecting a letter for me if there is a reply. She knows where I wrote to and why. I should have trusted you with the task, but I did not wish to burden you further and risk your father's wrath if you should be discovered.'

She nestled his head to her bosom. 'Oh, James, what fools we are! It is true, love can blind you — but not to each other; to the rest of the world. We must be more careful.' She felt him chuckle and released him.

'I need to breathe too, although I could not think of a more pleasant way to go. Sophia, if I have true wealth, I will need that head of yours to be at its sharpest, for I am not used to it. You will have to be my guide and my partner in all things. I have no wish to gamble, squander, or flaunt it, but to use it to secure our future so we shall never be poor. And when Napoleon is defeated, which he will be, we shall celebrate with my limited 'family' and make their lives more amenable too.'

'You are a good man, James Dalesman, and I love you as much as I always have.' She kissed him with so much eagerness that, as she nearly tumbled atop his body, it was only his squeal that broke the moment when he felt the pain shoot down his leg.

'Sorry,' Sophia said as she instantly stood upright.

'You are one passionate woman, and it is just as well that I nurse a broken limb, or right now you would be a fallen one. I am not so strong as to resist. I never have been when it comes to my Sophia.' He smiled up at her.

She took a step backwards, laughing. 'Read your books, and I will go and see to my duties. You sleep well this night; and if any banshee visits you, scream out, and I will come and rescue you with my crop in hand.' She flicked it harder than she ever would against any horse and left James laughing, his eyes filled with life and his colour returning.

* * *

Sophia did not return to him for some time. The house still needed her time, as arrangements had still been left to her and she had much to think about. She had had one thought bothering her and decided it was now the time to act, and enlisted the services of a junior maid who rarely came above stairs to reorganise her drawers. This innocent act, which was passed off as an opportunity for the girl to expand her skills in the absence of the upper housemaids, meant that Sophia had two complete outfits to hand to pack in a trice, one for day wear and one for travel. Then, should she need to leave at short notice, she would be prepared. It was done also without Cynthia's knowledge. Sophia was pleased to have them there, but she then realised that James could not travel for some time; and if avoiding a match meant removing herself to the abbey over at Beckton for a time, then she would. The nuns were always kind to her when she arranged for the produce of their gardens to be chosen for the Hall to supplement their own when needed. She had also given extra to them to help them when theirs failed. Sophia was at least doing something to determine her own destiny.

When Cynthia returned, they exchanged greetings as if nothing had happened between them. Clearly Cynthia was a more practised actress, or deceiver, than Sophia thought she ever could have been. A strange prick of conscience momentarily touched her, for had she not been deceptive herself in her younger years to have what she wanted? She had lied to achieve her desire, which had been time with James.

She was glancing out of the window of the morning room when her father and Lucas Huntley returned. Sophia admired his poise and had to admit that he cut a fine figure. She went to greet them as they entered the stable yard. The day was warm and sunny, so it was good to step outside.

'You are a vision of perfection, as always,' Huntley said as he dismounted, leaving his horse to the stable lad. He had no need of the mounting block that her father was using.

'And you are too generous with your compliments as always, sir,' she replied. It was hard not to show that his attention humoured her and gave her pleasure.

'That is why you are so becoming; you really believe that I exaggerate the truth.'

He always had the correct response to her comments. She liked his quick wit; it meant that she could spar with him easily.

'I have had fresh lemonade served in the orangery,' she said as her father joined them.

'That is a lovely thought, but you two go ahead. I will join you shortly,' he said, and patted her arm before walking into the Hall.

'It appears we have been abandoned. Why not take a turn around the walled garden and enter the orangery from the outside rather than going back through the dusky Hall? It is such a beautiful day, after all, and I am sure you are tired of hiding within. Dare to feel the sun caress those beautiful cheeks.' Lucas gestured towards the walled garden that ran the length of the Hall's west side from front to back and then joined the orangery at one corner.

'What a splendid idea,' Sophia agreed, for she could not see the harm in it at all. His words were more poetic than those James used. But then one was born and bred as a gentleman, and the other raised and taught to read the Bible by his father, who was a gentle soul although he laboured hard and could read the spreadsheets of the day and the Good Book. But his education, although to be complimented for one of the lower order, could hardly compare with such a man as James Huntley. No! *Lucas* Huntley. She smiled back at him as if to see him anew. Why was she confusing these two very different men in her head?

He smiled back at her and stepped aside, so that she led the way through the old wooden gates and into the garden, where immaculately laid beds of flowers and vegetables were such a pleasing sight to view.

Sophia heard the gate being latched behind her and glanced back. Lucas was walking along the outer path that followed the wall around the rectangular flower beds. She was going to walk straight to the orangery, but he stopped her.

'Let us take the air and enjoy the day. We can walk the full circuit. It is so rare that we can talk to each other in private.' He breathed deeply. 'Ah, pure air, away from the city stench — perfect! As are you,' he added.

Sophia glanced around them, ignoring his remark, but liking it nonetheless. With the Hall overlooking the gardens, and despite the fact that there were no gardeners working at that particular hour, she could not see any harm in doing as he said. So she began walking. Each plot was edged with green oak sleepers and alternated between beautiful flowers such as lobelias, roses and nasturtiums, and seasonal vegetables, not to mention the strawberries that fed the Hall's residents and guests.

'So what have you been up to with Father these past few days?' Sophia asked.

'He has been showing me his stock of sheep as well as his horses.' Lucas walked slightly ahead of her, standing in the shade of the arbour. 'He really has an impressive selection of bloodlines going back generations in both cases. I think we will be able to make a really good arrangement.'

Sophia thought it odd that he used the word 'stock'.

He reached up and picked a wild pink rose that was woven across the frame of honeysuckle. The perfume of the flowers in this shaded stretch of the walk was heady and almost intoxicating. As Sophia entered the shade, he presented the flower to her with a flourish of a bow that would have made any dandy proud.

Sophia giggled, like Cynthia she thought, as she dipped a curtsey and took it from his hand. But as she did, he held onto her fingers and led her deeper into the middle of the fragrant tunnel. It was only then that she realised she was completely hidden from the view of the Hall. Even if they were watched from a window, they would not be seen.

'We must join my father and Cynthia in the orangery,' she said, and stepped past him; but he encircled her waist with his arm and gently but firmly brought her into his embrace.

'Lucas!' she gasped. 'What do you think you are — '

Her words were lost as her lips were smothered by his mouth. His moist and eager tongue penetrated her mouth in a way that was more urgent or aggressive than James' exploratory kisses had been. Those ignited her soul with warmth that grew and overwhelmed. Lucas's were stealing her breath; were needy — no, greedy. Her chest heaved as she struggled with his arms, trying to push him away. He loosened his grip on her and allowed her to stand up straight again, steadying her and still holding on to her hands.

'You shame yourself and me!' Sophia said, and tried to pull her hands free from his; but his grip was firm.

'No, my pretty Sophia. I merely give you a taste, a promise of the delights that you and I will experience together.' He let her hands drop and gestured they should continue their walk.

'I do not know what you mean,' she said, whilst brushing her skirts down with her hands so that they did not appear at all crushed or creased by his assault.

'I think you do, Sophia, for you cover your tracks well.' He gestured to her actions. 'Rather than running screaming to your father for my ungentlemanly behaviour, you are more concerned about your appearance and what it might reveal to him.'

He was smiling at her, but she did not care for his manner or inference. She quickened her step, but he stopped her again by holding her right arm above the elbow in his left hand as he stood before her.

'Let go of me before you insult me again and I do say something that will destroy your reputation further and ruin your business arrangements up here.' She glared at him, but was resolved not to show open anger or fear.

'There is no need or danger of that.' He looked at her curiously for one moment. 'You are aware that my reputation has a dent in it. That is interesting. So you care enough for me to have bothered to find out if there is a stain on my character,' he said, and looked quite humoured.

'It is common knowledge that you deserted your fiancee,' she said defiantly.

'Is it?' he murmured, and looked slightly taken aback. 'Your mama should have told you not to listen to idle gossip.'

'I never do. I listened to clear and concise fact,' she railed.

'Very well. Did they also tell you why I did this terrible thing?' He cocked his head to one side.

She hesitated.

'No, of course they would not, because only I and the lady in question actually know the truth of it. So as it is nobody else's business, I will not bother your ears with it in case your lips part with the clear and concise truth of it to a third, fourth or fifth party.'

Far from acting like a cad, he was defending the reputation of his ex-fiancee. 'You insult me in an unfair and cruel way, sir,' she said, trying not to show him that he had gained any of her respect.

'I did not mean to insult you.' He shrugged. 'It is my way, Sophia. I am a man who speaks his mind, and I go all out to have what I want in life. I have no doubt that you are as a maid should be, but I am glad that you are not weak in nature or given to a fit of the vapours. I need a woman who has a strong character and bearing, and who can accept a full and active married life. You are that woman; and do not fear, for you are part of our arrangements. So,' he continued, freeing her arm, 'let us join the family, composed and in a friendly way. We do not want to upset them, do we?'

'I am not aware of any arrangement, and that is no way to behave to a lady, and one who you should be showing a great deal of respect to. I am not part of Father's ancient stock blood line to be bought at auction!' She walked on.

'I like that spirit.' He raised his voice slightly, a couple of steps behind her.

'It is not yours to like or hate.' She

continued walking.

'Not yet, my sweet, but soon,' he said, and then appeared in step at her side, so when they could be seen in the daylight they were to be walking together in unison.

'Admit it at least to yourself, you found my kiss exciting,' he said to her with an exquisitely light air that would have looked from a distance as if he was commenting on the mass of roses that covered the wall.

'I admit nothing!' Sophia said in response.

He laughed as if she had made a quip. 'You do not deny it either, though,' he replied whilst waving to Cynthia, who had had the manservant open the orangery doors to admit them both as they approached.

There was not time for Sophia to formulate an answer, which was just as well, as there was none she could give. Deep inside her, she knew that the answer was — yes! It had been exciting, but it had also been dangerous, not loving and sharing. It seemed to be an action that promised more reckless acts. Would they be loving, though? Were they to stake a claim upon her? Would she be treated roughly, rather than . . . ? Sophia had to prevent a smile crossing her lips because she remembered all too well the heightened feelings that James aroused in her every time they were remotely intimate. He did not grip her; he held her in a warm embrace, and then the exploration of each other's bodies had begun. He was the only soul who had that intimate knowledge, and she treasured the thought.

She re-entered the shade and was aware that Cynthia's eyes were studying her as the men talked about the lieutenant's recovery.

'He will be able to join us down here tomorrow,' her father announced.

Cynthia clapped her gloved hands together. 'That is good news.' She smiled at Sophia, who merely nodded back in a gesture of acknowledgement and carefully poured herself a glass of lemonade, being careful not to let the wave of excitement that swept through her cause her to spill one drop and give her feelings away.

11

The next day began with a flurry of activity as James was carried down the stairs carefully in his basket chair by Brent, Robert Judd, and two young hands from the estate. He looked fresh and wore one of her father's burgundy silk dressing gowns. It suited him and, with the contrasting black collar and cuffs, had a military appearance to it.

By the time they had had lunch, he was looking very weary and insisted that a nap in his chair would be sufficient rest, no need to return to his bedchamber.

Sophia could tell he had had enough of it and was happy to at least be able to look at the outdoors whilst on a level with it. He was not used to a life of confinement. She thought it was just as well his spirit had not been trapped within the body of a woman, with all the constraints placed upon them. She left him to his peace and then slipped inside the study.

'Father, I need to talk to you.'

He was seated at his desk as she expected, head down, and lost to his thoughts.

'Why, what have you done now?' he said in a serious voice; but then when he glanced up at her and smiled, she was relieved that he was just teasing her.

'It is about your plans with Mr Huntley,' she began.

'Indeed, I would like to talk to you about the same. So we are in an accord for once. Who do you think should go first?'

Sophia was keen to jump in, but for once in her life she didn't. Instead, she smiled sweetly back at him and said, 'Father, you must, of course. But I would ask that you then listen seriously to my comments and consider them, please?'

'Very well, that seems fair to me.' He

nodded and gestured she should sit in the chair opposite him at the desk.

Sophia did this but instantly felt small in the large leather chair. Perhaps that was his intention, as she noticed that his seat seemed elevated compared to hers.

'Please begin, Father,' she said and, instead of sitting upright and awkward in this reduced position, she leaned comfortably back into the chair as if he was about to read to her or orate some tale to entertain. One thing Sophia knew she must do or be lost was maintain control of her temper and her manner. Now was not the time for childish tantrums. This conversation could determine the course of her life, make or destroy her and James' dreams, or send her to a foreign land in the hands of a man who was not shy in making plain what he would do to her as his wife. Sophia listened to every word her father uttered.

'Old Huntley is a lifelong friend of Cynthia's family, and as such, they have my hospitality and utter respect.' Her father shrugged as this was an undeniable fact that was not in question. It also implied he, or they, owed the man in some way.

Sophia nodded.

'They have a plan to raise a vast number of sheep on land they are purchasing in a far-off country which has a very different climate to our own. It is a land they know little of. This seems a fine plan — daring, cunning and not without risk.'

He waited for her to respond before continuing. She nodded again.

'Lucas Huntley Senior is very keen to move this plan along, as the purchase of their acreage has been approved. It seems he wishes to send Huntley Junior out there to oversee the initial arrivals and set up the farm. He will need good strong hands as well as the beasts themselves.'

She nodded at him, her lips sealed.

'Sophia, unless you have become struck down with some affliction that cannot prevent your head from rocking, please stop it.' He placed the palms of both his hands face down on the desk, and she realised he would finish the conversation there and then if she didn't join in. Silence was not an option.

'Sorry, Father,' she said, and sat upright with her fingers interlocked on her lap. 'I was listening to you.'

'I realised that. So tell me, what do you think of Mr Huntley Junior so far this visit?' he asked her, and this time he was sitting back, one hand and forefinger resting his chin.

'He is quick of wit, confident, and is always making every effort to be charming to me,' she answered honestly.

'So what is he not?' he asked. 'The truth?'

'Honest in his affection for me and is in his intentions.' She saw her father's expression harden at her comments.

'And what intentions has he shared with you, Sophia?' he asked, and she realised that she had been lured into his trap. He had said as much, as he was not going to speak further until he knew her thoughts. She was flattered and pleased, because her father loved her enough to care what they were.

'He thinks I, like your sheep, am hardy and capable of surviving the crossing to this raw land and no doubt breeding him strong heirs in time.' She was being blunt.

Her father raised a brow at her choice of words.

As she spoke, she chose words that deliberately aligned Huntley's opinion of her in terms of the livestock he was purchasing.

'He does, does he? And when, pray, did he have the opportunity to share these thoughts with you?' he asked, and leaned forwards.

'Yesterday, Father, when we walked in the walled garden,' she again answered honestly.

'Do you concur with them?'

'No, Father, for I have no wish to

venture so far from you, Cynthia or my home. Besides . . . '

'Besides what?'

'Besides, he does not love me in the slightest, but I believe he finds me attractive for all the reasons previously stated, plus the money that would come to him upon my wedding and down to him in time as an heiress.' She softened her voice for the last comment.

'Love!' he sighed. 'Always love first with women.'

'Yes, because if we are to submit our body and life to the will of men, then love at least makes our futures palatable, if not enjoyable.' She blushed slightly on saying this, as the intimacy she had shared with James did indeed make her happy. But he should not know of this, and she should not be aware of those emotions and desires, even though they were very much present in James' case. 'Otherwise, we are like a flock of sheep, and to market we go . . . ' Sophia bit her lip; the passion of her words was beginning to show.

'Woman, do not lecture me. I know what you read.' He yawned.

'I did not mean to, sir,' she said automatically when his tone hardened, for she did not want to be banned from reading her choice of book.

'You were doing so well, Sophia, yet I am 'sir' again. Never mind, you may go.' He waved her away.

Sophia felt a wave of panic rise through her. He had discovered what he had sought knowledge of — her thoughts — but she had no understanding of his own intentions. This, like her life, was not fair!

'Father, what do you intend to do?' she asked, and leaned into the desk, her eyes moist and pleading. Her resolve to remain detached and calm hung in ruins.

He stroked her cheek with one finger. 'Sophia, I will do what I always do. I will look to the future and what is best for you. That is all I have ever done.' He stood up.

'Go and read to the lieutenant, and I

congratulate you on your control, for not once was he mentioned as a reason to prevent the marriage to Huntley. You are learning well from my dear Cynthia.'

'Father!' she said. She too stood up and was going to step towards him, but he put a hand up and waved her away.

'Go, Sophia. Do not say more to me now, or say anything of this conversation to anyone else, or you may work against your own interests. Do something you rarely have done in the past and trust in me and my judgement. Not another word. Now be gone!'

Sophia left the room; she walked out of the open front door and leaned against a column, breathing deeply. Did that go well? Could she trust him? Time must be her friend, for she needed more of it. James needed to heal, and she needed to slow Lucas Huntley and his vast plans down. But how? She looked to the sky. But how?

When she looked back down, she saw a rider coming at a gallop down the drive. Whatever now? she wondered.

She waited until he dismounted almost before the exhausted animal stopped and ran up the steps.

'Whatever brings you here?' she asked the rider.

'I have an urgent message for Mr Lucas Huntley,' he said, and pulled out a letter in which he gripped tightly.

'I shall give it to him.' She held out her hand.

He looked apologetically at her through a tired face. 'I am sorry, miss, but I have been instructed to give it to him directly.'

'Then follow me,' she ordered. 'Judd! Judd!' she shouted, not at all happy that she had been rebuffed by the man.

'Yes, Miss Sophia?' He ran out of the servants' corridor.

'See to this man's horse,' she ordered, and led the rider straight into her father's study and explained what he was about with one outpouring of explanation, as she forgot to knock first.

The man delivered his missive.

'Find Lucas, Sophia, and send him to

me,' her father ordered.

The man looked as though he was fit to drop, but until his missive had been delivered he would not get drink, food or rest.

Sophia found Lucas with James playing chess in the orangery. It was a game that James was learning fast, and he had now bettered his teacher, much to Huntley's annoyance. He was a man who obviously liked to win and was not a generous loser. James had noted this and shared it with Sophia. So the next few games he had deliberately thrown to the lesser man. James had told Sophia that once you knew your enemy's weakness, you should pick your time well enough to use it. Lose if it gave him false confidence, then strike.

This statement in itself was revealing because it showed how shrewd James was and also that he viewed Huntley as his enemy, to be beaten, at least where her affections were concerned. The thought pleased her, because Lucas made her feel like his prey, whereas

James wanted to cherish her.

'Mr Huntley, a rider has arrived and is in Father's study. He says he urgently needs to see you.' Sophia stepped back as he abruptly rose, nearly knocking the pieces on the floor as he jarred the chess table.

'Thank you,' he said, but stormed past her.

James gestured ever so slightly with his head that Sophia should follow him. She did, but neither the gesture nor her intent had been missed by Cynthia, who pretended to be absorbed in her needlepoint.

Sophia followed Huntley into the room. Slipping in, she stood with the door closed behind her.

The man held out the letter that Huntley ripped open. Her father waited whilst he read it.

'You may go, man,' he said to the rider, who Sophia opened the door for; but she stayed. 'Go to the kitchens and tell them I said you are to be given food and drink. We will call you later if there is to be a reply today.' The man nodded and left.

Sophia still held the door handle. Her father shot her a disapproving look, but she merely raised an eyebrow at him, showing she intended to stay. Huntley had his back to her and so would not be aware of her presence.

'It appears I have a new problem. My father has taken ill. His heart, apparently. So I must return before the day is out.' Lucas sighed and scrunched up the letter into a balled fist with white knuckles.

'I am sorry to learn of this. Do they say how long it will be before he recovers?' her father asked.

'They do not know.' He waved his arms upwards and let them fall as if devoid of hope. It was indeed a theatrical gesture, Sophia thought ungraciously. 'And I am to return without a settlement being agreed. Will you grant me the proposal I seek so that I can go to him and fill his tired heart with joy?' Huntley stood square before him.

'I will do better than that, my dear Lucas.'

Sophia's heart raced. What was he about to say?

Her father stood and placed two reassuring hands on the younger man's shoulders. 'I will ride back with you. We shall deliver our good news together!'

Huntley hesitated. 'There is no need for you to exert yourself. You are needed here, sir.'

'Nonsense, man! I am needed at this time elsewhere. Sophia and my estate manager will do an admirable job here in my absence, won't you, Sophia?' her father said, and Huntley's head shot around.

She was not sure what that look was, but she did not care for it. Was it anger, frustration, doubt or annoyance that she should be privy to man's conversation?

'Yes, Father,' she replied.

'Good. So go and tell the rider that he will no longer be needed and can return once he and his horse have rested.'

'I should send word that we are both coming,' Huntley said, and tried to turn away, but her father stopped him. 'I do not want any more shocks to strike his heart further. This is already too much. I cannot bear to be the reason for his failing,' he said.

'No need for thoughts like that, my good man,' Sir Kenneth confirmed. 'We will see that all is well. Besides, that man looked done in. If that is the state of the rider, then the horse must be too. We will return together. I insist.' He slapped Huntley on the back, and Sophia quickly did as she was bid.

12

Sophia entered the servants' corridor, making her way down to the kitchens. It was a strange feeling of déjà vu, for she had not ventured down here since the day she ran away from her mama's screams, passing the very spot where she was caught and carried away over Brent's shoulder. She heard light-hearted chatter amongst the clatter of pans and pots being moved around in the kitchen, and so she put her memories aside and headed straight there.

One voice was that of Mrs Gribbins, the other was unmistakably that of James, while another she supposed was the man who had brought the message. She entered under the low stone arch and was greeted by at least four shocked faces, as there were two maids working at the sink and table.

'Keep working, girls. I have not come down here to rebuke anyone,' Sophia said politely.

The girls did, adding extra vigour to their tasks that made Sophia smile; they were obviously in awe of her presence.

James was seated by the fire with a warmed jug of mulled wine in his hand. The rider made his excuses and left immediately by the stable yard. Sophia saw he had made the most of his opportunity by the empty plate and tankard that were left behind. He did not even wait to be dismissed.

Mrs Gribbins lifted her head and smiled. 'You caught me reminiscing with the brave lieutenant here. Sorry, miss,' she said, but the apology was lame, as was the slow way she made to get up from her comfy chair by the range.

'You have much to catch up with.' Sophia looked at James, who appeared to be well warmed through. 'Were you feeling cold?' she asked him, trying not to show concern.

'No, not at all, but I have not been able to see Mrs Gribbins yet, and so I made my way down the servants' stairwell with the aid of Judd.'

'Well it's not my place to venture upstairs, is it?' The woman sniffed, but there was an edge to her voice that Sophia could not understand. Why should she have been invited upstairs? Then she realised how close these two people were to each other and felt a strange pang of guilt that she had cut the woman out, albeit unwittingly.

'Girls, go to the dairy and bring some fresh cream and butter in. Not much, just a small jug and a half dish of butter,' Mrs Gribbins ordered, and the young kitchen hands made themselves scarce.

James looked up at Mrs Gribbins, whose hands had settled on her hips. 'Please do not say anything, Mrs G,' he said, resigned to the apparent fact that the woman intended to.

'You drink your wine and do not try to stand, lad,' Mrs Gribbins told him, and then presented herself before Sophia. 'That man,' she said, pointing at James, who was shifting his weight in the chair as if he wished to stand or run, 'is worth far more than that Huntley fellow any day of the week. You, Miss Sophia, are right for him and he for you, but the other is a waste of a — '

'Mrs G!' James snapped, and she glanced at him and nodded as if she would rein in her words for his sake.

'Well, as I was saying,' she continued; but James looked up as if he knew there was no stopping the woman once she had something on her mind. 'That other gentleman is no gentleman, and I would not want to see you hitched to him, Miss Sophia. And I know it's none of my business, and speaking out I could be turned out like young James here was. But he made a play for our Millie, the scullery maid, and that ain't right and nor fair either. The girl ran to the woods, and it was all I could do to get her to come back inside. He won't get no chance to finish what he started. So I'm going to see your father, and if he turns me out, then shame on him and the lot of you!'

'Mrs G! Enough now,' James insisted. 'I will tell him,' he said.

'No, you won't,' Sophia said. 'For if you do, the outcome could be dire for you.' She looked at Mrs Gribbins. 'For us. You have reason to want to discredit him.'

'Fine.' Mrs Gribbins began to untie her apron.

'You will not speak with him either. I shall do so before they leave, for a message has been brought to say that old man Huntley is ill abed and needs his son to go to him.'

'Very well. It is just as well someone does!' Mrs Gribbins snapped back; but it was Sophia who responded.

'Enough, Mrs Gribbins! I do not need telling who is good for me and who is not. I am quite capable of deciding that myself. Look after James, and I will see that word is delivered to the right ear. Now, this girl, did he . . . I mean, is there any chance that she may have a . . . ?' Sophia's stance and resolve were fading.

'No, miss. He was interrupted before that happened, but he would have, and he has frightened her right good,' Mrs Gribbins explained.

'You will make sure the girl has rest and some of what James is having.' Sophia stopped, as Mrs Gribbins' shock was instantly apparent.

'That's me best — '

'Whose best wine?' Sophia said, and saw the grudging admission in Mrs Gribbins' face that it belonged to the Hall.

'Aye, well, you're right. But James is family, and — '

'This girl needs raising above the lowly position she feels that she has been pushed into. So for one day at least, she will have a fine cooked meal and a glass of wine placed in front of her, and one of your delightful puddings. It will not erase the memory of her abuser, but it will provide good sustenance, which will help her recover, knowing she has my word that it will never happen again.'

Mrs Gribbins nodded her agreement. 'Very well. You always were a good lass, if not a little headstrong. Right for my James,' she added, but Sophia raised a warning finger at her.

'Quite enough, Mrs G,' she said.

'Yes, ma'am,' she answered and curtseyed.

'James, I will see Father. You stay safe, here and I will tell you later what is happening.'

'Yes, and I you.'

Sophia raised a questioning eye at him. 'You have your letter too?' she asked.

He nodded, not giving anything away. But as she saw the delight in those eyes that she could read so well, she nodded at him. In her heart she felt all would be well, would work itself out somehow; but she must speak with her father. Sophia left them.

Huntley apparently did not know the difference between desire and sheer carnal lust for what he wanted and felt he had the right to take. Well he couldn't, and would not have her or anyone else in her household. She would stop him.

She burst into the study, but her father was not there. Instead, Cynthia was standing by the fireside with an unfolded letter in her hand. For a moment, Sophia thought it must be James' reply, but then she saw quite clearly that it was in fact scrunched up. It was the one Huntley had discarded carelessly into the fire grate; but he had been in too much of a rush and had not made sure the flames or embers had caught it, and so it had only charred around the edges.

'What does it say?' Sophia asked, and stood beside Cynthia as the woman held it out for her to read.

Junior,
Why have you not sent word that you have sealed the deal? Do not fail

me again. If you must leave the blasted sheep, we can get them elsewhere as Merinos may be best, but get the filly. For God's sake, use that brain of yours. Tell them I am weakening and need this match to give me hope. I await good news. Was your last fiasco not enough to discredit us? Of all the heiresses you chose, you had to lay with one who had a disfigurement, making heirs impossible! Make sure that you compromise Baxter-Lodge's whelp and have the deal sealed.

Senior.

'Has Father left?' Sophia asked.

'No, not yet. You see, whilst you were chasing James, I came in here, found and shared this with him. He is currently preparing to leave with Huntley, but he has more to say to Senior than the man is expecting.' Cynthia cocked her head on one side with a self-satisfied smile spreading across her face.

'There is something else. He tried to have his lecherous way with a young maid called Millie,' Sophia explained, and was about to leave when Cynthia's reply stopped her.

'He may have, but that will not cut much sway with him, as it is a perk of owning a house like this. Men abuse their positions, and she would not be the first woman to succumb to the lust of a handsome, wealthy man with a honeyed tongue.'

'But Father would never . . . ' She looked at Cynthia's calm expression.

'My dear Mrs Gribbins was young once,' Cynthia explained.

'No!' Sophia could not take this latest revelation in.

'Oh, yes, and he regrets it dearly, because she lost the child he gave her, your half-brother. And then she could have no more, which is why the lad James is so special to her. He found a child who needed a mother whose father worked on the estate, and so they were moved close, and the lad worked in the stables and was nurtured by Mrs Gribbins.'

'How would you know this when you were not even here?' Sophia could hardly believe her ears.

'Because he told me. You see, Kenneth and I do not have any secrets between us, unlike you and your father.'

Sophia left, filled with thoughts and emotions that would make her heart pound and her head burst if she did not find her father before he left.

13

Sophia ran upstairs to her father's bedchamber, but he was not there. She was about to return, hoping against hope that if he were in the stables, she would be able to keep him there for a few moments. The thought of him having been intimate with Mrs Gribbins, who had never married but was known respectfully, like a housekeeper would be, as 'Mrs', made her stomach turn over. But if this man was capable of attacking a young girl, and Huntley's father was complicit in her own downfall and entrapment, then her father might well be in danger.

It was only when a hand grabbed her arm and swung her around that she was aware that Huntley was still upstairs. He had dropped his bag by his door as he was leaving. He pulled her back into his room, covering her mouth with his and pushing her hard against the wall.

Her breath was rapid as he released her, but she could not pull away from his weight. He held her hands down at her sides and quickly slipped them behind her back, leaning into her.

'I will scream,' she said, panic building, fear almost palpable.

'Go on, for then you and I will be compromised, our tryst and affections laid bare, our union hastened; and that I can hardly wait for,' he said.

Repulsed, she head-butted him, sending him backwards with his hand reaching to the bridge of his nose.

'You bitch!' he yelped. But she was out of the door, down the stairs and into her father's arms before he reached the top of the stairs.

'What happened?' he asked. Cynthia looked on from the study doorway.

'He tried to fulfil his father's orders,' she explained, then stood back from her father and stared up at him. 'The man is a cad, and abhorrent. He tried to rape one of our maids,' she explained, then glanced at Cynthia.

'No, I did not. The girl tried to improve her station in life and begged me to take her away, but I refused and then her heart broke, poor deluded creature.' Huntley was calmly coming down the stairs. 'Should we go?' he asked her father, ignoring her completely.

'No, we shall not! You treat my daughter abysmally, and you expect me to seriously offer her hand in marriage?' He shook his head. 'You are beneath contempt.'

'Not at all. You see, I have been busy whilst playing chess. We have been discussing strategies, have we not, James?' Huntley looked to the corridor, where James was reappearing, wheeling his basket chair forward.

'Indeed, we have,' James admitted. 'You see, for Lucas's daring plan to work, he needed a witness who could whisper in the right ears that he had seen Sophia willingly enjoying the close affections of Lucas Huntley. If such a rumour were to reach the circuit of the colonel in an officers' mess, then Lucas had deduced that no one would marry her, save for a lowly lieutenant who had risen in the ranks. Something you would never wish upon your only offspring. So to avert this downfall, the answer is simple: you let them wed, and the stain and disgrace is taken away to the New World with them. He would pay me a sum of twenty guineas to play along,' James said as Huntley's self-satisfied expression grew into a grin.

'So, Father-in-law, your Sophia will be mine or will be disgraced — the choice is yours.'

Sir Kenneth glared at James. 'You would do this after everything I have done for you?' His fists were balled, and Sophia thought that he might kill James with one blow, but she did not doubt that it was James who played a cunning game here and that soon it would be checkmate to him. She did not doubt him for a second.

Know your enemy's weakness, and

when the time is right — strike. He had just struck the man down, and Huntley was so arrogant he could not see it. How she loved James so.

'Yes, I played along, but you have no need to abide this scoundrel any longer in your house, for he is beneath the lowest creature I have ever seen in any conflict. I would never betray Sophia or yourself,' James declared.

'You bloody fool!' Huntley yelled at James. 'Was it more money you wanted? Was that it?'

'No.' Huntley made to come at him, but James held a pistol that he slipped out from underneath the dressing gown he wore. 'You see, I have no need of your money, for I have been busy making my own these last five years. Whilst you whored, I fought and earned reward.' James made no apology for his use of language.

'You are from the dung heap and will forever be so. Money will not buy you the rank and education of a gentleman,' Huntley declared.

'If you shoot him now, we will all give witness he attacked you,' Cynthia said. Sophia gasped, as she was not at all certain Cynthia's words were meant as a bluff.

Huntley stood back. He grabbed his coat and bag and backed out of the front door, where his horse was already saddled. Her father stood still.

Cynthia giggled. 'I didn't mean it, and James would never commit such a cowardly act, but that coward judges people by his own lowly standards.' She shrugged and went back into the orangery.

James placed the gun back at the side of the chair. He looked up at Sir Kenneth. 'It isn't even loaded. I thought to have it with me in case we came to blows. I am disadvantaged at the moment.'

'We need a port or a sherry. Come into my study.'

Sophia wheeled James in, but she stayed and poured out three glasses of port. Her father looked at her in surprise; she handed a glass to each, but then sipped her own and rested on the window seat.

'What a mess this is. He may say what he likes, and our name will be tainted.' Her father shook his head.

'That he won't,' James said confidently.

'What makes you so sure?'

'Because in order to finance the purchase of the land, which has just been accepted, he had to draw on funds raised against the sale of property in Newcastle and in London. They have a debtor's note outstanding for the sum of a thousand pounds, which if called in could stop the money going through.'

'I fail to see what that has to do with anything. Who owns this debtor's note?' Sir Kenneth looked at Sophia, who shrugged.

'You do, sir. I purchased it.' James smiled at them.

'You? How can you purchase such a thing, and how do you know to?' Sir Kenneth was staring in amazement at what he was hearing.

'I had been drinking with him in an inn before I arrived. He has a loose mouth. He was saying how he was about to 'bag him a filly'.' He looked at Sophia. 'His words, not mine. I did not know who he meant until I discovered he was coming here. I wrote immediately to my broker in London to find out what I could. I have a tidy sum in accessible bonds. I wanted to gift you this debt for your leverage as a thank-you for the kindness you have showed me and Mrs Gribbins over the years,' he added, and Sophia saw her father's cheeks colour at the mention of their cook. So she knew Cynthia's words were true.

'Has she been keeping in contact with you about my affairs?' He almost cringed at the use of the word.

'Yes,' he said.

Sir Kenneth sat down on the edge of his desk. 'Well you know that you have the debtor's note, but Huntley does not, so what good will it do if his mouth becomes loose on the journey home?

He passes many inns en route,' he said, and looked crestfallen.

'Because his father does know. He will have received a letter to inform him who owns his debt now, and that you will be in contact with him shortly.'

'Are you intending to purchase my favour, my daughter, for the price of this debtor's note?' Sir Kenneth railed.

Sophia stood instantly, but James put up his hand to stop her from speaking.

'It is a fair question and assumption.' James looked at Sophia. 'Such a jewel could never be purchased. I would ask that you allow me to stay here until, as Doctor Aimes claims, I can walk unheeded again. And if I still do not impress you, then I will purchase a higher commission if the wars drag on, and prove my love for her all over again.'

'James, no! You nearly died once already. Father, you cannot let him do this. He has done everything to be a good friend to me and to this family. Is it not enough that he has earned position, wealth and has been injured?

Would you send him back again?' Sophia pleaded.

'I need time. We all need time. This has gone badly. Huntley will pay for the abuse he has meted upon my household. The money will be repaid to you with interest, for you acted quickly and in my interest; but never presume to do so again and acquire anything in my name, or you will not be able to stand again in this life. Do I make myself clear?' He raised his voice so much that even Sophia nodded.

'Yes, sir,' James said as any good soldier would to his commanding officer.

'Now leave, the pair of you; and the same terms of your stay are to be kept. Break them and I will not even consider your union.'

'Yes, sir,' they both chirped, and James left them with Sophia holding the door. Before she left, she looked back at her father, who stared blankly back at her.

'Mrs Gribbins?' she said.

'Do not even risk a conversation into areas which do not concern you. Do I make myself clear?'

'Yes, sir,' she said, and left without looking back.

14

'James! How marvellous!' Everyone stood and clapped, and Cynthia squealed as she saw him enter the morning room without his stick. Two and a half months after he'd limped into the Hall, James was standing tall. It felt so good to him. This was a moment in his life he would never forget. How lucky he was to have kept the leg at all; but to be able to walk straight again unaided was all down to the care he had received here.

Sophia looked happy to see him, but there was sadness in his heart. For what excuse now was there for him to stay longer? He had mended; not well enough to ride and return to his duties if he so chose, but enough to stand tall again.

Sir Kenneth stood up. 'You are walking straight and proud. Good man!' he said, and came to personally greet him with a hug.

'It is all thanks to your generosity and kindness, sir.' James was genuine in his comment as he knew, left as he was, he would have been a cripple for life. *How do you ever repay such a debt?* he thought. *Not by running off with the man's daughter against his wishes.*

'Not to mention your courage and patience in the healings and the restorative properties of Mrs Gribbins' special chicken soup, no doubt,' her father jested, and Sophia noted that same tone of affection she had heard months earlier in his voice when he mentioned the cook's name and wondered if there was more to his tryst than Cynthia had realised.

'We need to talk, sir,' James said.

'Well, you two sit and talk with my dear Cynthia. I have something that I have to do.' Sir Kenneth looked away, and James felt rejected after building his hopes up for this moment. As if sensing he had been rather abrupt, Sir Kenneth added, 'We'll talk, but later, man. The women have much to say, as always.' He let out what sounded like a choked laugh as he left.

★   ★   ★

Staring at the rhubarb in the cottage garden at the back of the Hall, Sir Kenneth was in deep thought.

'Give you a penny for them,' Mrs Gribbins said, and stood alongside him. 'You have the look of a troubled man, sir.'

'You haven't got a penny to give, wench,' he said, and heard her chuckle in return. It was a good, hearty, honest laugh.

'That's where you are wrong, because James has seen me right, and Rob and even Brent,' she added.

Sir Kenneth looked at her. 'Then why are you all still here? You could be free of me, of the estate, of your chores. He has a generous spirit.'

'You are a dote, sir,' she said, and turned to face him. 'This is your home and ours too. You are our 'master', and we love you because you treat us all right. We share your wealth because you allow us to live well here. None of us want to leave. We want for nothing. Where would we go? And young James is a lovely man. She could do no better.'

'You know I cannot say yes to him. He has no heritage, woman.' Sir Kenneth's voice almost broke with emotion.

'No, but neither had I, had I Ken? Our love was thrashed, but did it ever go away?'

'I loved my wife . . . '

'Aye, I loved her too, for it was not of her doing she was matched like a prize bull to a cow.'

'You are crude woman,' he snapped, but did not walk away.

'Aye, and you laughed at that once and fell in love with my honesty when all around you sat on circumstance. Do not let two hearts break again, Ken. He has money.'

Sir Kenneth spun around to face her. 'From where? He must have stolen it.'

'No, man, he found it buried. Like how Samuel Pepys buried his cheese when London burned. Aye don't look surprised. You used to tell me all that useless stuff, and I remembered it.'

'Oh Mrs G,' he said, and put an arm around her, drawing her close. 'The older I am, the more regrets I have.' He sniffed.

'Oh, Ken. You had the love of a beautiful wife and lost her tragically, but your new wife adores you and you her. You should not blubber so,' she gently admonished.

'What of you alone in the kitchens?' he asked guiltily.

'Oh, I'm rarely alone. And besides,' she whispered, 'Brent and I have been more than friends for some years. But we're not allowed are we?'

It was Sir Kenneth who looked shocked. 'Then you shall be from now on,' he said, and his eyes watered up again.

'Oh, Kenneth, please stop blubbering in front of the servants!' Cynthia's voice snapped at him. His arm dropped to his side as if he'd been caught in an illicit affair.

'Sorry, ma'am,' Mrs Gribbins said.

Cynthia smiled. 'Don't be. You should not regret a thing. You tell Brent your good news. Now take hold of yourself, Kenneth. Let those two young people live and love their lives together. It matters not.'

'She is my heir, Cynthia. Tradition dictates . . . ' Sir Kenneth said, but his words were not heartfelt and drifted off into nothingness.

'Yes, I know, and she may not be for much longer. For you will have another child by Christmas, and if it is a boy then she will not be your heir, will she? So let them be engaged to each other and declare it proudly to the world.'

'Oh, joy! I'll make some of me soup.' Cynthia and Sir Kenneth laughed as Mrs Gribbins ran back to her kitchen.

Sophia and James entered the garden to find out what the squeal of delight was for. Sir Kenneth's eyes were still watering, and he tried to compose himself as wave after wave of good news seem to put at rest years of guilt and secrets.

'Whatever is wrong, Father?' Sophia asked.

'Nothing, nothing. I am to be a father again, and you two are to be wed!' he said proudly, and swept them into a big hug.

Cynthia looked on and shook her head. 'Men,' she whispered, and winked at Sophia's delighted face as he held tightly to James, who had all but crumpled too.

MOLLY'S SECRET
CHLOE'S FRIEND
A PHOENIX RISES
ABIGAIL MOOR:
THE DARKEST DAWN
DISCOVERING ELLIE
TRUTH, LOVE AND LIES
SOPHIE'S DREAM
TERESA'S TREASURE
ROSES ARE DEAD
AUGUSTA'S CHARM
A STOLEN HEART
REGAN'S FALL
LAURA'S LEGACY
PARTHENA'S PROMISE
THE HUSBAND AND HEIR
THE ROSE AND THE REBEL
FREEDOM'S FLOW
MADDIE MULLIGAN

THE SIGNET RING

Anne Holman

Resigned to spinsterhood, Amy Gibbon is astounded to receive a proposal of marriage from Viscount Charles Chard upon their very first meeting! Love quickly flares in her heart, but Charles is more reticent — he needs an heir, and this is a marriage of convenience. Determined to win her new husband over, Amy follows him to France amid the dangers of the Napoleonic wars, where he must search for his father's precious stolen signet ring. Can true love blossom under such circumstances?

THE LOST YEARS

Irena Nieslony

Upon returning from their honeymoon in Tanzania, Eve Masters and her new husband David are quickly embroiled in chaos. When a hit-and-run accident almost kills them both, David develops amnesia and has no recollection of who Eve is. And then she pays a visit to his first wife — to find her dead body slumped over the kitchen table, with herself as the prime murder suspect! Will Eve be able to solve this tangled web, and will David remember her again — or will the villains win for the first time?

SAFE HAVEN

Eileen Knowles

Taking shelter from a snowstorm, Giselle Warren revisits an isolated holiday cottage, expecting it to be vacant — and walks straight into someone's home instead! Blake Conrad, the owner, has moved in after splitting with his girlfriend. In rocky circumstances of her own with her fiancé, who she suspects wants to marry her purely for her money, Giselle has been hoping for solitude in which to gather her thoughts. But this chance meeting with Blake will change both of their lives forever — after she makes him an incredible proposition . . .

A TOUCH OF THE EXOTIC

Dawn Knox

From India to war-torn London to an estate in Essex, Samira's life is one of rootlessness and unpredictability. With her half-Indian heritage, wherever she goes she's seen as 'exotic', never quite fitting in despite her best efforts. To add to her troubles, her beauty attracts attention from men that she's not sure how to handle. But when she falls for handsome RAF pilot Luke, none of her charms seem to work, as it appears his heart is already bestowed elsewhere . . .

A LORD IN DISGUISE

Fenella J. Miller

When Lord Edward Stonham kills his opponent in a duel, he is forced to flee and take on a false identity. As country gentleman Edward Trevelyan, he recruits Penelope Bradshaw, the eldest daughter of a well-born widow fallen on hard times, to be his housekeeper. While they are initially secretive about their personal circumstances, they soon become confidantes. But Edward is not in a position to offer for Penny's hand in marriage, so they can never declare their love. Are they prepared to ignore propriety in order to be together?